ZEKE

A CHRISTIAN ROMANTIC SUSPENSE

OATH OF HONOR

LAURA SCOTT

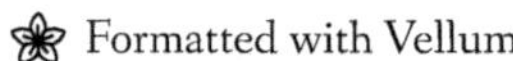 Formatted with Vellum

Sienna Reynolds stopped abruptly when she caught a glimpse of the envelope propped against the front door of her rental home. Just like all the other notes she'd received, her name was written in italic lettering followed by an exclamation point. Exactly the way her name appeared on the playbill of her show, *Sienna!*

Turning, she scanned the quiet White Gull Bay neighborhood. At eight o'clock at night, several homes had lights glowing from windows, but she didn't see anything out of the ordinary. She wondered if any of the neighbors had Ring doorbells that may have picked up an image of the man who'd left the envelope.

Not that she needed a camera. She already knew her ex-husband, Josh Allenton, had left this note, just like all the others. If not him personally, then someone he'd paid to do the deed.

Swallowing against a wave of dread, she bent to pick up the envelope, then punched in the numbers on the keypad entry to go inside. She forced a smile when she saw her nanny, Taylor Templeton, sitting in the living room reading a book. "Hi, how was Bailey?"

"A sweetheart as usual." Taylor's brow furrowed when she saw the envelope. "Another one? Really? I didn't hear a thing."

"Yes, but it's okay." She moved to the kitchen to set the envelope on the counter. The note inside would likely be some variation of the previous messages.

I know where you are.

You can never escape.

I'm watching you.

The notes wouldn't bother her so much if it wasn't for her two-year-old daughter, Bailey. She knew Josh had recently decided he wanted joint custody of their daughter, something she would fight against until her dying day.

Hopefully, it wouldn't come to that.

"Sienna, you can't keep ignoring them." Her nanny gestured toward the note. "You need to call the police."

"That would be playing right into Josh's hand." They'd had this argument before, and nothing had changed. The moment she called the authorities, Josh would use the information against her. He'd insist on taking custody of Bailey to keep the little girl safe from whatever crazed stalker had targeted Sienna.

No way was she going there. Yet the fact that Josh had found her here in White Gull Bay, Wisconsin, so quickly was concerning.

She needed to do something. She'd returned to her hometown to kick off her solo Christian singing tour, *Sienna!* And while Josh could easily discover she was in the Milwaukee area, he should not have been able to find her rental home.

Pressing her hands on the counter, she stared down at

the envelope. Then she quickly ripped it open. The words were written just like the last ones.

I'm coming for you.

Suppressing a shiver, she shoved the note away. Earlier today at rehearsal, she'd considered calling her brother's best friend, Zeke Hawthorne. If Luke were still alive, he'd have moved heaven and earth to protect her and Bailey.

But Luke had died during a military training mission eighteen months ago. Bailey had been six months old at the time, and Sienna had already started divorce proceedings against Josh after the third time he'd struck her in the face in a fit of anger. The only good thing about being physically abused by her now ex-husband was that she'd been granted sole custody of Bailey.

For now. Unfortunately, Josh was now fighting against that ruling in court. Thanks to his parents' wealth, he had been able to secure one of the best family law attorneys in the state of California. He'd buried her in legal proceedings until she'd wanted to scream.

She knew Zeke was a cop, as he'd mentioned working on some sort of tactical team when they'd briefly chatted at Luke's funeral. It was almost as if she could hear her brother in the back of her mind telling her to call Zeke. To get support from someone within law enforcement to fight back at Josh.

"Sienna?" Taylor's voice brought her out of her reverie. "You shouldn't wait until something bad happens. You need to call the police sooner than later."

Taylor had a right to be concerned. Her job as Sienna's live-in nanny meant she was at risk of being hurt by Josh too.

"You're right." She blew out a breath and pulled out her phone. She and Zeke had exchanged contact information at

Luke's funeral, so she quickly found his name and made the call before she could talk herself out of it.

"Sienna? What's up?" Hearing Zeke's voice in her ear nearly brought tears of relief to her eyes.

"Hi, Zeke, I, um, hate to bother you, but would you have time to stop by? I'm renting a place in White Gull Bay." When he didn't immediately respond, she quickly added, "If you're too busy, I understand. I know this is rather unexpected. If tonight's not good, we can meet up tomorrow or some other day."

"I'm not busy, Sienna. Just surprised to hear from you. I can be there in fifteen minutes, if that works?"

"Perfect, thanks. See you soon." She lowered her phone, hoping she hadn't caught Zeke at a bad time. It had been eighteen months since she'd seen him, and he was likely dating someone or could even be engaged by now. Not married, as she felt certain he would have invited her to the wedding.

Wouldn't he?

"I thought you were calling the police?" Taylor asked with a frown.

"Zeke's an old family friend and a cop." A wailing cry came from the nanny cam speaker, so she brushed past Taylor to check on her daughter. Bailey was usually a good sleeper even despite the frequent trips from one city to the next.

"Mama." Bailey rubbed her eyes, then lifted her arms. Sienna didn't hesitate to pick her daughter up, cuddling her close. Closing her eyes, she prayed God would keep her daughter safe.

Especially from Josh.

She lowered herself into the rocking chair, holding her daughter while willing her to go back to sleep. After ten minutes, Taylor poked her head into the room. "Sienna?" Her voice was a whisper. "I think your cop friend is here."

"Thanks." Moving gingerly, she rose and set Bailey in the portable crib. Thankfully, the little girl didn't wake up. She left the room, closing the door behind her.

"I'll let you talk to him alone," Taylor said. "And I'll listen for Bailey too."

"I appreciate that." Sienna headed to the front door of the rental, opening it just as Zeke was about to ring the bell. "Hi, Zeke. Please come in."

"Sienna." His broad smile eased her worry. He looked freshly showered, the faint hint of aftershave clinging to his skin. He gave her a one-armed brotherly hug and kissed her cheek. "How are you?"

"Great." She forced a smile, feeling guilty for reaching out because she needed his help. When he arched a brow, she added, "Okay, I could be better. Please have a seat. Would you like a soft drink?"

"No thanks." His gaze was serious now, and he didn't sit on the sofa until she'd dropped into the closest chair. "I get the sense something is wrong."

There was no point in pretending there wasn't. "I hope I didn't interrupt your evening plans."

"You didn't. I was just finishing up at the gym." Zeke leaned forward, pinning her with a direct gaze. "What's going on, Sienna?"

She hesitated, then stood and quickly grabbed the envelope and note from the counter. Bringing it back to the living room, she handed it to him. "I'm in town for a week and am planning to kick off my first solo tour this weekend." She grimaced. "I came home from rehearsal tonight to find this propped against the front door."

His scowl deepened as he read the note. Then he looked up at her. "Who sent it?"

"I believe my ex-husband is responsible." She twisted her fingers together. "That's not the first note I've received, and I suspect it won't be the last. My biggest concern is how Josh found me so soon. Bailey and I just arrived yesterday."

Zeke scowled, setting the note and envelope aside. "Maybe you should start at the beginning."

"You probably remember I filed for divorce from Josh," she said. "I told you about that at Luke's funeral. What I didn't mention was the reason I left was because he began to physically abuse me. I had to wait until he struck me hard enough to leave a bruise, then I took pictures and went to the police. Thanks to the evidence of abuse, I was granted sole custody of Bailey."

"He hit you?" Zeke's expression turned to stone. "You should have told me that right away."

She sighed. "It's not an easy thing to discuss. Besides, that's not the issue anymore. Josh has a new lawyer and is fighting for joint custody. These threats are his way of paying me back for breaking up our singing duo. After I went solo, I switched to Christian music, which ironically has skyrocketed my career." She'd learned so much about God and faith in the past year. And she was humbled by the gifts God had graced her with.

"That's wonderful news," Zeke said, and she could tell he was truly pleased for her. "I'm so proud of you."

"Thanks, but God is the one who granted me this gift. And I'm still very afraid of what Josh will do." She bit her lip, then forced herself to continue. "My ex is a manipulative narcissist. I never should have married him, but that's what I get for being young, foolish, and naïve. The point is, he's not one to take my success over his failure lightly."

"I see." Zeke nodded slowly. "We need to call the police to get this note on record."

"No." She rose and began to pace, trying to find a way to make him understand. "Josh wants me to call the police. He wants the entire world to know I'm in danger from some strange stalker. I guarantee that he'll have an alibi for the time frame in question and will act all innocent and concerned, as if he still cares about me."

"But, Sienna . . ."

"No, this is exactly how he operates. This is all part of his master plan." She whirled to face Zeke. "He'll use the perceived danger as an excuse to take Bailey." She used air quotes. "'To keep her safe.'"

Zeke stared at her for a long moment. "Okay, I can understand why you won't want this information to get out in the press, but I have connections within the Milwaukee Police Department. We can investigate this under the radar."

She frowned. "Maybe. But that will only last while I'm here in town, right? My next show is in Chicago. And I'm headed to Louisville after that."

"I see your point." His gaze turned thoughtful. "But that just means we need to find and nail this guy while you're here." Zeke glanced around the rental. "I'll start by sleeping on the sofa."

"What about your girlfriend?" she asked, trying and failing to sound casual.

"No girlfriend or fiancée or any one special." He gestured to the envelope and note. "We might want to see if we can lift prints off this."

"Don't bother." She was secretly thrilled to know Zeke wasn't involved with anyone. Not that she was interested in a personal relationship. One bad marriage was more than enough to last her a lifetime. Still, it was nice to know she wasn't intruding too badly on Zeke's personal life. "I had a private investigator do that on the first note about a month ago. There was nothing to find."

"We'll try again anyway," he persisted.

"Only as long as there isn't an official police report that can be used against me." She would not give in on that point. "Seriously, Zeke, I don't want anyone other than you and my nanny, Taylor, to know about this." From this point on, she would not even keep her manager, Dirk Green, in the loop.

"Okay, but my sticking close is bound to raise some suspicions," Zeke pointed out.

That was true. And it was also one of the reasons she was so glad he wasn't involved in a personal relationship. "I know this is asking a lot, but would you consider pretending to be my fiancé? That way, you can be here and backstage without raising suspicion."

Zeke stared at her for a long moment before offering a crooked smile. "I'd be honored."

"Thank you." Tears pricked her eyes, and she turned to quickly brush them away. Oh, she knew Zeke was only doing this because he was Luke's best friend. But she was grateful for his support anyway.

She silently prayed they could get to the bottom of this soon. Before she had to face Josh and his high-priced lawyer in court. The mere idea of being forced to hand her precious little girl over to Josh made her sick.

She vowed to do everything in her power to prevent that.

ZEKE HATED KNOWING his best friend's sister feared for her life and that of her little girl. It made him furious to think about Sienna being physically abused by her ex, and he was determined to make sure the guy didn't get anywhere near her. Or their daughter.

He planned to stick to her like glue. Thankfully, he had his duffel in his SUV, a replacement for the truck that had gotten shot up a few weeks ago. He'd walk the property tonight to see what he was dealing with.

Tomorrow, he'd talk to Rhy, his boss at MPD, about the situation. When that was set, he'd get Sienna an engagement ring.

Just thinking the words made him flush. Sienna couldn't know about how much he'd wanted to ask her out back when he and Luke were in high school. His best friend had made it clear his baby sister was off-limits. Zeke had honored Luke's wishes, especially since Sienna was way out of his league. Even back then, she'd won several state championships for singing.

Now she was here in Milwaukee about to kick off her first solo tour.

They weren't high school kids any longer. After everything Sienna had been through, the last thing she needed was for him to mention his former crush on her. He rose to his feet. "I'm going to start by scouting the area outside. I'll need the code to get back in."

"Of course." She rattled off the four digits, then followed him to the front door. "I'll introduce you to Taylor when you're finished. She's my live-in nanny."

He turned to gaze at her. "Are you sure you can trust her?"

"Yes, Taylor's been wonderful. She takes good care of Bailey." Sienna answered without hesitation, but he wasn't about to take anything at face value. Not when it came to protecting Sienna and her daughter.

For now, he'd keep his suspicions to himself. "I'll be back in about fifteen to twenty minutes. Stay inside with the door locked until you hear from me. I won't knock but will call you when I'm finished."

"Okay." She closed the door behind him. He waited until he heard it lock before moving off the front porch. There was a definite chill in the cool autumn air, and leaves crunched beneath his feet as he moved around the house.

The area was decent, nice homes that weren't sitting on top of each other in a neighborhood with a notably low crime rate. Yet those facts hadn't prevented someone from approaching the house to leave a threatening note on the doorstep.

I'm coming for you.

The veiled threat set his teeth on edge. Resting his hand on the butt of his service weapon, he made his way around the house. The landscaping was nice, but he found himself wishing there were fewer trees and overgrown bushes. Normally, he'd be impressed by how the owners had created a backyard that provided privacy from the neighbors.

The excess foliage provided far too many places where a perp could remain hidden from view. This early in fall, there were still plenty of leaves on the trees, providing additional cover. Those leaves that had fallen to the ground made it difficult to find footprints as well.

Not the most ideal situation, but not the worst either. He could understand Sienna's desire to avoid hotel rooms. Especially since she was here for a full week. He assumed her first show was Friday, but he would need to get a copy of her schedule to know the dates, times, and locations of each show.

He was surprised he hadn't heard about Sienna's scheduled performances before now. Granted, he'd been knee deep in several big operations, including one where his fellow teammate Jina had been abducted by a stalker.

Still, he felt way out of the loop.

After clearing the property, he walked to the street to make sure there weren't any cars parked nearby. Finding nothing, he turned to head back, stopping to pull his duffel from the back seat. He and the rest of his teammates had gotten in the habit of carrying a change of clothes and toiletries, as they often ended up in situations that required an overnight stay. Tonight was proof of that. As he made his way to the front door, he called Sienna to let her know he was coming in.

He found her hovering near the door. Earlier, he'd ruthlessly squashed his instant attraction to her. Now, it wasn't nearly as easy to keep his distance.

"Everything is fine." He managed a reassuring smile. "No sign of anyone lingering nearby."

"Thanks for checking." She stepped back, shivering despite her thick burgundy sweater. "I, uh, made up the sofa for you. Sheets, blanket, and pillow."

He nodded, touched by her thoughtfulness. "Thanks. I appreciate that."

"There are three bedrooms." She tucked a strand of her long, dark-brown hair behind her ear. "I'm in the master with Bailey in the room next to me. Taylor is using the other guest room."

"Sounds good. What about the lower level?" He'd noticed several deep window wells, indicating there was additional living space in the basement. "Mind if I take a look?"

"Oh, sure. The basement is finished off, and there are a few additional bedrooms down there, along with a third bathroom if you'd like to sleep in a real bed."

"No, I'll stick to the sofa." He had every intention of being close at hand if someone did try to get in. "I just want to be sure everything down there is locked up tight."

"Of course." Her smile didn't reach her blue eyes. "The stairs are in the kitchen."

She led the way, opening the basement door and flicking on the light. Edging past her, he descended the steep staircase. The ceiling over the stairs was so low he had to duck his head.

There was a large game room, complete with a pool table and dart board. Then he found two additional bedrooms, each with a deep window well leading outside. He understood the need to have the windows with access to the outside in case of a fire, but he didn't like them. He double-checked that those windows were locked, wishing there was a way to secure them better.

The rooms were far enough from the stairs that he couldn't be sure he'd hear the breaking glass if someone tried to get in. He scowled, considering how being here in a rental house wasn't much safer than a hotel room. But this wasn't the time to broach that subject.

Tomorrow would be soon enough.

He mounted the stairs to the main level. Sienna was sitting at the kitchen table cradling a cup of tea in her hands.

"Would you like something?" She eyed him over the rim. "I tend to drink licorice root tea with honey to soothe my throat between performances."

"I'm fine." He nodded to the cup. "Does it work?"

"Seems to." She took another sip, then lowered the cup. "I'm trying to think of the logistics of our arrangement. I know you work during the day, and I'm sure Bailey, Taylor, and I will be fine while you're at work. But if you could give me your schedule, I'd appreciate it. Oh, and I hope you don't mind, but I'll probably have to call my manager to let him know that I—we're engaged." She blushed. "That way, he can get the word out."

"You don't want your manager to know about the notes?"

"No." She stared down at her tea for a long moment. "Dirk is a great guy, but he's always pushing me to do interviews and other marketing events. For now, I'd like to keep him in the dark. Thankfully, he has only one TV interview with the Milwaukee Morning show, early Thursday."

"Speaking of schedules, I need yours too." The morning show gig was interesting. It was Monday night, so that was three and a half days from now. "And don't worry about my job. I have plenty of vacation time coming. I'm sure my boss won't mind if I take a week off."

"Are you sure? I don't want to put you out any more than I already am." Her gaze was troubled. "I feel bad taking advantage of our friendship. I just . . . wasn't sure what else to do."

"Hey, there's no one I'd rather spend time with on my vacation," he assured her. He didn't mention his teammates would be shocked to hear about their engagement. Especially since he couldn't tell them it wasn't real. He reached over to take her hand. "Trust me, Sienna. I'll keep you and Bailey safe."

"I know you will." She looked as if she might say something more, but then she pushed her tea aside and stood.

"Good night, Zeke. I'll get you a copy of my schedule first thing in the morning."

"Good night." He stood and waited for her to disappear down the short hallway leading to the three bedrooms. Then he doused the lights and made his way to the sofa. The sectional was soft and long enough to accommodate his six-foot-two-inch frame.

Not that he expected to get much sleep. It took a few minutes to adjust to the sounds of his strange surroundings. The fridge hummed, the ice maker dumped ice cubes into the tray at regular intervals, and a clock ticked with each passing minute.

He must have dozed because a strange sound had him jerking awake. Bolting off the sofa, he grabbed his weapon from the nightstand and moved to the window overlooking the front of the house.

Then he heard the thudding sound again. His heart squeezed in his chest as he softly made his way across the room to the back of the house.

Straining to see through the darkness, he thought he saw a shadow behind the overgrown lilac trees. Then he heard the crash of breaking glass. Swiveling away from the living room window, he ran to the kitchen in time to see the glass scattered on the floor and the brick sitting on the kitchen table.

With a note wrapped around it.

CHAPTER TWO

The sound of breaking glass woke Sienna from a deep sleep. The first real rest she'd gotten since the notes had started. Frowning at the late, or rather early, hour of four in the morning, she drew on a robe and hurried from the room, stopping abruptly to avoid smacking headlong into Zeke.

"Get dressed." His tone didn't encourage an argument. "Someone tossed a brick with a note through the window. We need to get out of here."

Taylor's door opened, revealing her sleepy nanny. "What's going on?"

"Taylor, this is my cop friend Zeke. I—we need to pack our things." She knew they should have left the moment she saw the note but had thought they'd be safe enough with Zeke standing guard.

And they had been until now.

On cue, Bailey began to wail. Turning from Zeke, she quickly opened the door and hurried over to her daughter. "Shh, it's okay. Mommy's here."

"I'll get dressed, then help pack Bailey's things," Taylor said.

"What can I do?" Zeke asked. "We can't stick around for long. The police may already be on the way."

She nodded in understanding. Officers responding here would file a police report, which was the last thing she wanted. "Will you hold Bailey?"

"Gladly." He moved closer to take the little girl from her arms. She hoped Bailey wouldn't fuss; sometimes she didn't like strangers. Thankfully, the little girl snuggled against Zeke's broad shoulder. The way she never could with her own father.

Swallowing hard against the lump in her throat, she returned to the main bedroom. Her suitcase was huge, mostly because of the various dresses she needed for her three performances, so it took several minutes to get everything tucked back inside. Then she lugged it out into the hallway, joining Zeke.

He looked surprised to see her large suitcase but didn't complain. "I'll take that out to my SUV and Taylor's too."

"Then I'll take Bailey." She gently took the toddler from his arms, then followed him outside. "Don't forget to grab the car seat."

"Understood." Zeke scowled. "Wait inside, okay?"

She ducked back inside the rental house, as Taylor finished packing Bailey's diaper bag. After what seemed like forever, they had everything stored in Zeke's SUV. After placing Bailey in the car seat, she joined Zeke up front, leaving Taylor to sit beside her daughter.

That's when she noticed the brick sitting in an evidence bag. "This is what came through the window?"

"Yeah." Zeke's brow furrowed. "We need to figure out a place to stay that even your manager doesn't know about."

"Like where?" Taylor asked from the back seat.

"I'm not sure." Zeke navigated the small neighborhood,

putting distance between them and the rental house. "We'll find something. In the meantime, you need to let your manager know to pay for the window to be repaired ASAP."

Pulling her phone from her purse, she called Dirk. He didn't answer right away, and when he finally did, his voice was thick with sleep. "Now what?"

"I'm sorry to bother you at this hour. A brick came through the window of the rental. I need you to get it repaired tomorrow morning."

"Are you hurt?" Now he sounded concerned.

"I'm fine, and so are Taylor and Bailey. I just need you to do this for me, okay? And keep it out of the news."

"Yeah, sure. I'll take care of it." He paused, then added, "Is there a problem?"

"No problem, I have a feeling this was nothing more than a couple of kids goofing around." She strove to keep her voice even. She debated telling him about her new engagement to Zeke now but decided to wait. "Thanks, Dirk. I appreciate your help. We're moving to a hotel for tonight just to be on the safe side."

"Keep in touch and don't forget your TV interview is this upcoming Thursday morning."

As if she could forget something like that. "I'll be there. Thanks again." Before he could say anything more, she ended the call.

"You really think he believes a kid threw that brick?" Zeke asked, his tone skeptical.

She shrugged. "I hope so. If there has to be a police report, I'd rather the claim is related to petty vandalism than any potential danger to me."

Taylor soothed Bailey as the toddler fussed. Sienna turned in her seat. "Try giving her a bottle."

Nodding, Taylor rummaged through the diaper bag. "I made one just in case."

"Thanks." She turned to Zeke. "Where are we going?"

He glanced at her. "There are a few options. I'm leaning toward the City Central Hotel. They have suites available that will meet our needs. And it's located in downtown Milwaukee, as I assume that's where you're performing."

"It is." She hadn't even thought about her next rehearsal. "The City Central Hotel sounds like a plan. Thanks."

He looked as if he wanted to say more but didn't. Probably because Taylor was sitting behind him. Her plan to introduce Zeke as her fiancé had seemed like a good idea last night. Now, she was having second thoughts.

For his sake more than hers. He'd said he wasn't involved with anyone and that he could easily take vacation time, but this was obviously a huge imposition. One he was putting up with only because he and Luke had been best friends in high school.

She noticed Zeke was heading west, which didn't make any sense if the City Central Hotel really was downtown. "Where are you going?"

He shrugged. "We're taking the scenic route."

It took a moment for her to realize he was winding his way around the city to avoid being followed. Which only added to her guilt. She'd gotten several decent hours of sleep but doubted Zeke could say the same.

Was she being foolish not to report the notes and the brick incident to the authorities? Just the thought of Josh using the information against her sealed her decision to stay silent. She turned to look at her daughter, grateful to see Bailey had finished her bottle and had drifted off.

If she didn't need the money and hadn't already signed a contract, she'd be tempted to turn her back on this tour and take Bailey someplace where they could hide off-grid.

Unfortunately, not responding to Josh's legal motions could result in her losing custody of Bailey, too, so that wasn't an option. All she could do was pray that the court outcome would be in her favor.

Pray that the judge would see through Josh's manipulative actions.

Yes, she absolutely had to stay the course. Even if that meant imposing on Zeke's kindness. Blinking back tears, she tried to look on the bright side.

It was nice to be home, even just for a week. The move to Los Angeles seven years ago had seemed like a good idea at the time, especially as she and Josh had gotten their record deal.

Now, she dreaded having to return.

"Hey, we'll be at the hotel soon," Zeke murmured, covering her hand with his.

"I know." She managed a wan smile. "I don't have anything major going on today. I only rehearse every other day when I have upcoming back-to-back performances."

"I imagine you need to save your voice," he said.

"Yes." She gripped his hand, drawing strength from his presence. Calling Zeke had been the right thing to do. There had to be a way to make it up to him, even though she knew any attempt to reimburse him monetarily would be rejected. She'd have to think about how to make sure he understood how much she appreciated him.

Ten minutes later, he pulled into the small parking lot of the City Central Hotel. She was surprised to see it was relatively close to the courthouse. A sobering reminder of Josh's latest attempt to fight for custody of their daughter.

"Wait here while I go in and grab the keys," Zeke said.

She nodded, glancing back at Taylor. The minute Zeke was out of the car, Taylor leaned forward. "He's so handsome," she whispered.

"Yes, he is." She was not immune to Zeke's charm. But she wasn't looking to get involved again either. Battling Josh took too much time and energy. Between her work and taking care of Bailey, she didn't need other complications. "He—uh, we're going to pretend to be engaged. That way, he can accompany me to the music hall and hang around backstage without raising suspicions." She grimaced. "Plus, he promised to work on finding the person responsible without putting everything in a public access police report."

"Engaged?" Taylor echoed in shock. "Wow, that's a big request. Do you think that's necessary?"

"Yes." She shifted her gaze to her daughter. "Nothing matters but protecting Bailey."

"I guess it can't hurt to have a cop hanging around." Taylor's gaze reflected her concern. "You know I'll support you in any way I can."

"Thanks for that." Taylor shouldn't have to worry about being in danger too. And if things didn't settle down, she'd let the nanny go and find some other way to work around her daughter's needs.

The responsibility of completing her tour while caring for her daughter and Taylor was staggering. Leaning on God's strength was helpful, but so was having Zeke at her side.

They could do this. They had to. Failing to protect Bailey would crush her.

IT TOOK LONGER than Zeke anticipated to get the baby, the nanny, and Sienna settled into the hotel suite. It was the largest suite the hotel offered and still felt small and cramped with the four of them inside.

Taylor disappeared into her room, while Sienna settled Bailey in hers. He was making a pot of coffee when Sienna returned. "If you'd like to get some rest, I can move Bailey out here."

"No need. Let her sleep." He gestured to the coffee. "I'm usually up early anyway."

"I am, too, except for nights I'm on stage," she confessed with a wry smile. "I find it hard to fall asleep after performing. My body is too keyed up to relax."

"I can understand that." He thought she was beautiful dressed casually in jeans and a sweater. He could only imagine how she'd looked all dressed up and singing on stage. "What about your nanny?"

"Oh, she's a morning person." She shrugged. "I think these notes are getting to her, though. She doesn't feel safe."

"I don't know much about babies, but I can help," he offered.

"I'm sure we'll be okay. Taylor has been with me for about three months now. I found her in Wisconsin. The notes just started a few weeks ago."

"What's Taylor's last name and date of birth? I'd like to run her through the system." He kept his voice low so the nanny wouldn't overhear. Just because Sienna trusted her didn't mean he was going to do the same.

A cop's motto was to consider everyone a suspect until cleared.

And that was especially true now.

"She came with stellar references," Sienna said with a frown. When he continued holding her gaze expectantly, she sighed. "Okay, fine. Taylor Templeton, her birthday is June 10 of"—she waved a hand—"I'm not sure. She's twenty-four. You do the math."

"I will." He jotted the information down and then reached into his duffel to pull out the laptop. By the time he'd finished verifying Taylor Templeton didn't have a criminal record according to the expanded search, considering her home address was in Madison, the coffee was finished.

"Told you," Sienna said, filling a cup for him. "She has a degree in early education, and I pay her a decent salary."

He didn't care what her salary was. Greed was still a motivator for many crimes. "I see the worst in people every day. Those who would hurt or kill others for a lousy few hundred bucks. Does your ex-husband come from money?"

"Yes, his parents, Alice and Tom, are extremely well off," she said with a frown. "But Taylor cares about kids. She wouldn't do anything to hurt Bailey."

He wanted to believe that for her sake. "Fine. What about the rest of your schedule?"

"I have it here." She scrolled through her phone. "I can send you the document. What's your email?"

He gave it to her, and a minute later, a message popped up on his screen. Thinking of her phone and the way she'd been found made him frown. "We'll have to head out to buy a few things once the stores open. A new phone for you is at the top of the list."

She looked as if she wanted to argue but then caught herself. "Fine. If you think that's necessary, I will, even though it's probably overkill."

The comment irked him. "Come on, Sienna, how else is your ex tracking you?"

"This phone is new since our divorce," she said. "I understand that phones can be tracked, but it's not like he even has this number. All of our communication since the final divorce hearing has been through our respective lawyers. I haven't spoken to Josh directly in almost two years."

"But he's rich, and you're famous," he said. "Your shows aren't a secret; we passed a billboard on the way here. Obviously, Josh knows you're in town."

She took a sip of her coffee, then sighed. "The shows have been well advertised, but I made the decision to come here several days early. I don't have any idea how Josh figured that out. Especially to track us to the rental house."

"From this point forward you don't tell anyone, including your manager, where you're staying." The more he thought about this situation, the less he liked it. "I don't even want him to know your new phone number. We'll keep the old one to use on rare occasions, and only after we're in a public place."

Her eyes widened in shock, but she nodded in agreement. "That works. I shouldn't really have to talk to him much anyway. He's in town for the shows, and I can arrange for all meetings to be in person at the venue."

It was a step in the right direction, but he still wasn't satisfied. There were too many ways this plan could fail.

Badly.

Scrutinizing Sienna's schedule didn't help. Today was wide open, but tomorrow afternoon she had a rehearsal scheduled and the following morning was the TV interview. Then Friday evening was her first live show, followed by another on Saturday night and Sunday night.

One day at a time, he told himself. When Bailey awoke, drawing Sienna's attention, he used the time to leave a message for his boss, Rhy Finnegan. He didn't like leaving the team in the lurch by taking vacation at the last minute, but Rhy always said family came first.

Sienna being his fiancée, fake or not, still counted as family.

Which reminded him about the need for her to wear an engagement ring. They'd get a new phone first, then the ring. Based on how difficult it was to get everyone out of the rental last night, he estimated the two errands would take half the morning.

Taylor emerged from her room looking freshly show-ered. The nanny quickly hurried over to help with Bailey. "Would you like me to make a bottle?"

"Thanks, and some cereal too." Sienna turned to him. "Would you mind grabbing the car seat? That will have to work as a high chair to feed her."

"Sure." He should have asked for baby furniture when making the reservation. "I'll see what the hotel has for us too."

As predicted, by the time they'd gotten a crib and high chair from the hotel and had their room service breakfast delivered, the hour was going on nine o'clock. He reminded himself that babies couldn't be rushed, but it wasn't easy to sit back and wait.

"I'd like to say grace," Sienna said, when Bailey was finished. She set the toddler on the floor with some toys to distract her.

"Of course." He bowed his head, thinking about how things had changed for Sienna since her divorce. She and Luke hadn't grown up attending church, but she'd found a home singing Christian music.

Nice to know it wasn't all for show.

"Dear Lord Jesus, we ask You to bless this food we are

grateful to eat. And we ask that You continue to keep us all safe in Your care. Amen."

"Amen," he echoed. After a heartbeat, Taylor did too. To help lighten the mood, he added Roscoe's favorite ending to each before-meal prayer. "Dig in."

Sienna smiled and took a bite of her veggie omelet. Taylor seemed to enjoy her scrambled eggs, giving Bailey a few to try. The way the little girl toddled around unsteadily made him want to cushion the place with pillows to soften her inevitable fall.

When Rhy returned his call, he rose to take it in the other room. "Hawthorne," he answered.

"What's going on, Zeke?" Rhy demanded. "I didn't even know you were seeing anyone, much less seriously enough to propose."

"Sienna and I have been friends for years but only grew more seriously involved recently." *Like yesterday*, he thought grimly. "I'm sorry to bug out on you at the last minute, but I'd like the rest of the week off."

"Yeah, I listened to your message," Rhy said. "When's the big day?"

The big day? Oh, the wedding. He fought a flash of panic. "She's a Christian musician doing several shows, so I'm not sure yet. I just appreciate you giving me this time off."

"Yeah, sure." He could tell by the sound of Rhy's voice that he hadn't fooled his boss. "You know we're here if you need us, right?"

"I do. Thanks. Later." He ended the call, but Rhy's comment gave him an idea. He quickly called Flynn. "I need a favor."

"Yeah, I heard. Don't worry, Grayson is covering your

shifts. Roscoe is still around, too, at least until Libby goes into labor."

With a wince, he realized he'd forgotten about Roscoe's pregnant wife due any day now. "Thanks, Flynn. What are you doing this morning? Any chance I can convince you to babysit a nanny and a two-year-old for a few hours?"

"Wait, if I'm babysitting the two-year-old, what's the nanny doing?" Flynn asked.

"No, Taylor, the nanny will take care of the baby. I just want you to sit here and keep an eye on things." He and Flynn as the two single guys on the team had gotten close over the past few weeks. "I'll explain everything later, okay?"

"Sure, why not?" Flynn sighed. "My shift doesn't start until three. I can hang around at the City Central Hotel for a while."

"Thanks. I owe you." He gave Flynn their suite number. "Text me when you get here."

"Will do. Should be there in fifteen to twenty. That's minutes, not years," Flynn joked, before ending the call.

Zeke couldn't help but smile as he returned to the kitchenette. In some ways, he had a feeling this week would feel like an eternity. At least until he had this guy tossing bricks and leaving notes in custody.

He finished his breakfast, then filled Sienna in on the plan. "I have my buddy Flynn stopping by here to watch over Taylor and Bailey while we run a few errands." He caught Taylor's curious glance, and added, "He's a cop too. We both work on the tactical team, which means we have special training that other police officers don't have."

"That sounds great." Taylor looked relieved by the news.

"Yes, thanks for arranging that," Sienna agreed. She

stood and scooped Bailey into her arms, swinging the little girl high and making her giggle. "That gives me just enough time to change her."

"I can do it," Taylor offered.

"It's fine. You'll have Bailey all to yourself soon enough." Sienna pressed a kiss onto Bailey's chubby cheeks as she carried her into the other room.

"She's a great mother," Taylor said, after they were gone. "I really hope you get the man responsible for this. Sienna doesn't deserve this. And from what I hear, her ex-husband shouldn't be allowed in the same state as Bailey much less have joint custody."

"I'll do my best." He didn't like making promises he couldn't keep. Yet in this instance, he had no intention of failing Sienna or her daughter. He turned to pin the nanny with a stern look. "I don't want you talking to anyone except me, Flynn, or Sienna. Not her manager or anyone else, understand?"

"Here." She pulled out her phone and handed it to him. "My life is in jeopardy too. Go ahead and take it."

He couldn't decide if she was clever and conniving or innocent and concerned. He didn't take the phone, thinking she'd need a way to get in touch with Sienna if Bailey got sick or needed something.

"Keep it for now." He offered what he hoped was a reassuring smile. "We'll get a replacement for you when we pick up new disposable phones. Flynn will be here to keep an eye on things."

"Whatever you decide." She sighed, then added, "I'm relieved Sienna has police support on this."

"I agree." He rose and stacked their dirty dishes together. Then he opened the door to set the tray out in the hall. Before he had a chance to hang the do not disturb sign, Flynn walked up the hall. "Hey, Flynn."

"Zeke." Flynn arched a brow. "Is it true?"

Wow, news of his engagement was traveling fast. "Yes." He wanted to tell Flynn the truth but held back.

"Congrats, bro, but how is it possible I didn't know you were dating anyone?" Flynn eyed him with suspicion, making him realize he may not be able to pull this ruse off with those closest to him. Especially Flynn.

"Look, I'll explain everything in more detail later, okay?" He kept his voice low. "For now, I need you to go with the flow."

Realization dawned, and Flynn nodded. "You can trust me. I won't let you down."

Zeke knew Flynn still felt guilty over the inadvertent role he'd played in letting Steele down in a situation earlier in the year. Since then, Flynn had gone above and beyond to support the members of the team.

"I know I can trust you." He lightly punched Flynn in the arm. "That's why I called you."

He quickly introduced Taylor and Sienna to Flynn. Even Bailey seemed to take his buddy's presence in stride. Zeke quickly got Sienna out of there, desperate to get to work.

"Phone first," he said, once they were seated in his SUV. "I hope you don't mind a disposable phone for the interim. We'll keep your phone off until we absolutely need it."

"Fine with me." She seemed to relax for the first time since they'd had to leave the rental house. "Flynn seems nice."

"He's great." He headed for the interstate. At this hour, traffic should be minimal. And it was, to a degree.

Until he caught sight of a dark-blue car keeping pace

behind him. He mentally kicked himself for not getting rid of the SUV before now. "Sienna? Hang on."

"Why?" The word had barely left her mouth when he jerked the wheel, taking the next exit without any warning.

His pulse spiked when the blue car followed. Not good.

"Zeke? Who is that?" Sienna's voice tightened with panic.

"Don't know. Just hang on." He focused on weaving through traffic, desperate to lose the blue car tailing them. Seconds later, the passenger window opened revealing the barrel of a gun. He shouted, "Down," as the sharp report of gunfire rang out.

CHAPTER THREE

Gunfire! Sienna huddled in the front passenger seat, sliding from one side to the other as Zeke zipped through the streets. Her mind grappled with this new threat. She'd never been exposed to this level of violence before. Guns and bullets were far different from anonymous threatening notes. Even the brick being lobbed through the window of the rental house hadn't been intended to kill her.

What had changed? And how had this car found them? Did the driver know Taylor and Bailey were back at the hotel? Flynn was there to guard them, but she didn't want her baby girl anywhere near the wrong end of a gun.

Closing her eyes, she prayed. *Lord Jesus, keep Bailey and Taylor safe in Your care! Guide us to safety!*

Zeke continued driving erratically, but she was thankful not to hear more gunfire. Had they lost him? How long would it take for the police to arrive?

She didn't want to get the authorities involved, but this recent event may leave them no choice. Lifting her head, she turned to look through the back window.

"I lost him," Zeke said, answering her unspoken question. "But we need to get a different vehicle. This is my fault. I should have swapped rides. My SUV was parked in the driveway of the rental property all night."

"You really think the guy who threw the brick saw your car and then found us by tracking your vehicle?"

"Yeah, I do. How else?" He shot her a quick look, before turning back to the road. "If your ex has unlimited funds, he could be paying someone, either a private investigator or a retired cop with no scruples, to track you down."

"I wouldn't put anything past him," she said in a low voice. "Josh is a terrible person. Yet shooting at us is a far cry from leaving notes."

"Maybe he's sick of playing around." Zeke's grim expression appeared carved in stone. "If so, he's bound to make mistakes. For now, I'm heading to Brookland. There's a car rental place there we can use to obtain a clean vehicle."

"I can pay for that," she quickly offered. "After all, this is my problem, not yours." She was beginning to feel guilty for dragging Zeke into this. This was a lousy way to pay him back for being Luke's best friend.

"Nope, we're not paying for anything under your name," he said. "Besides, believe it or not, we can use my boss's account to pay for the rental car. It's not the first time we've been in this situation."

That didn't make much sense to her, but she nodded. "Okay, but once this is over, I will reimburse you and your boss."

He gave a noncommittal shrug. But when she pulled out her phone, he stopped her. "No, you can't use that device."

"I need to check on Taylor and Bailey." She scowled. "I can't just sit here and assume everything is fine."

"Flynn has my number. He'd call if something happened." When she simply glared at him, he added, "As soon as we get the new car, you can call him from my phone. But consider this, Sienna. If your ex is tracking your phone, a call to your nanny could lead him directly to them."

That gave her pause. "Fine. I'll borrow your phone once we're in a new vehicle."

"Thank you." To her surprise, he reached over to gently squeeze her hand. She clung to it, wishing she didn't have to let him go. "I know how to stay off the radar. I need you to trust me on this, okay?"

"Okay." She might not like giving up control, but she trusted Zeke. More than she trusted anyone else. Even back when they were younger, Zeke had been an honorable guy. He and Luke had joined the military together, but Zeke had returned home after his first tour of duty to help take care of his mother who was battling stomach cancer. That was just the kind of man he was, putting others first.

The exact opposite of what she'd experienced with her ex-husband. How could she have been so stupid to marry Josh Allenton? Having a great voice didn't mean squat if the man was evil and manipulative.

She reminded herself there was no point in ruminating over her mistakes, of which there had been many. She was a different person now. One who'd welcomed God and Jesus into her life.

"Hey, it's going to be okay," Zeke said, sensing her inner turmoil. "I have a plan."

"I love a good plan." She strove to keep her voice light.

He smiled, then took the Brookland exit. She was somewhat familiar with that suburb as she and Luke had grown up in Greenland, which was only a few miles away.

So had Zeke. Looking at him now, she was even more impressed with the man he'd become.

She missed her brother. Their parents had split up, each getting remarried and having new, blended families. It wasn't that she didn't care about them, her parents were nice people, but over time, they'd drifted away. She and Luke had remained close. And it was telling that Luke hadn't much cared for Josh.

If only she'd listened to her older brother's warnings. But she hadn't. And despite how awful her current situation was, she would be forever grateful for Bailey.

Obtaining the rental car didn't take long. Their replacement SUV was a different make and model from Zeke's but still had plenty of room. Once they were settled inside, Zeke took a moment to pair his phone with the car's navigation system. As they left the rental facility, he hit the button to call Flynn.

"Yo, Zeke, what's happening?"

She breathed a sigh of relief when it was clear Flynn didn't sound concerned. "Hi, Flynn, it's Sienna. I just wanted to check in."

"Everything is great," Flynn assured her. "Taylor is in the bedroom putting Bailey down for a nap. Do you want me to have her call you?"

"No, that's fine." She glanced at Zeke, wondering how much he wanted to say.

"Flynn, we picked up a tail about ten minutes after leaving the hotel," Zeke said, taking over the call. "There were two people in the car; the shots came from the passenger side. Thankfully, we were able to shake them off. The shooter wasn't well trained; we weren't hit. And we just picked up a clean ride."

"Do you want me to move Taylor and Bailey to a new

location?" Flynn asked, all hint of humor vanishing from his tone.

"Not yet," Zeke said. "I think they must have tagged my vehicle once we were on the move. But I need you to stay sharp. If you see anything unusual, don't hesitate to get them out of there."

"Will do."

"Thanks, Flynn." Zeke ended the call, then glanced at her. "Feeling better?"

"Sort of." She sighed. "I believe Flynn will keep Taylor and Bailey safe. But I'm still upset we were found. Especially since we're not closer to nailing Josh for being the mastermind behind this."

"I'm with you on that." He gestured to the windshield. "We'll stop and pick up new phones at that store up ahead."

"Okay." Zeke was right to take things one step at a time. For the first time since they'd been fired upon, she relaxed.

Much like their visit to the rental car agency, Zeke knew exactly what he wanted in a disposable phone. She'd never used one before, but he was more than familiar with the various models. In addition to the phones, he picked up a laptop computer.

"Okay, we'll get these up and running soon," Zeke said when they were once more settled in the rental car. "We have one more stop to make before we head back."

"You're in charge." She glanced at their recent purchase, rather liking the idea of having an unknown phone number. Obviously, she couldn't hide from Dirk or the production crew at the music hall venue forever, but it was nice to be out of reach for a short while.

Then she frowned as Zeke headed to Greenland. "Where are we going? Is this a walk down memory lane?"

"Not exactly." He looked a bit flustered as he took the

next corner. "I have to pick up something from my place. It shouldn't take but a moment."

"Okay." She eyed the neighborhood with interest. "It looks different from what I remember."

"Lots of remodeling happening in these older and well-established neighborhoods," he said with a shrug. "I updated my mother's house too."

Her jaw dropped when he pulled into the driveway of his childhood home. "Wow, it looks completely different."

"Yes." He shut down the car engine. "Come inside. Like I said, this will only take a minute."

She followed him up to the back door of the house, looking around with frank curiosity as they entered. He was right, the small home had been completely renovated. There was no longer a wall separating the living room from the kitchen, and the staircase leading to the second floor had been opened up as well.

"You did a fantastic job, Zeke," she said with admiration. "I never would have recognized the place."

"I'll be right back." He disappeared down the hall, returning in less than three minutes holding a small ring.

An engagement ring?

"What . . . who . . . ?" She couldn't finish.

"It belonged to my mom. She and my dad loved each other for thirty years. As you know, my dad died first, then my mom passed a few years later." He held the diamond ring up. "If we're going to convince people we're engaged, you need to wear a ring. Although this may need to be resized."

She put her hands behind her back. "I can't wear your mother's ring. It's not right."

He gave her a quizzical look. "Why not? I can buy one if you'd rather, but I'm not sure how that's any different."

"No, of course, I don't want you to buy one." She obviously hadn't thought this through. Of course, she'd need to wear an engagement ring. Better that she borrow one, even though it felt wrong to wear something that belonged to his mother. "Okay, I'll borrow the ring for the week." She held up her hand. "Let's see if it fits."

Once again, Zeke surprised her by taking her left hand in his and gently slipping the diamond ring on the fourth finger. It fit perfectly.

For a long moment, she could only stare at the modest diamond ring on her hand. Then she cleared her throat. "It fits. Thank you."

"Anytime." His voice was low and husky, as if it shocked him to see the ring on her hand too.

For a fake engagement, this arrangement was beginning to feel all too real.

HIS MOTHER WOULD HAVE BEEN THRILLED, Zeke thought as he took a step back from Sienna. She'd told him to give the ring to the girl he loved. And he had.

Only Sienna didn't know it.

That was his problem, not hers. Besides, he didn't know her the way he used to. They were different people now.

Not to mention, she didn't live in Wisconsin any longer. Los Angeles would be the last city on the planet he'd choose to live. This was nothing more than a temporary arrangement.

"Okay, we need to hit the road." He forced himself to turn away, lest his expression betray his true feelings.

"Of course. I'm anxious to get back to Bailey." Sienna quickly followed him outside.

Once they were heading back downtown, he asked, "I'll need to look at the setup of the music venue prior to your first performance."

"Sure, we can do that anytime. There aren't any other shows scheduled this week." She frowned. "But I can't change the location or anything like that. I must honor the contract I signed."

"I understand, but there are probably security measures we can put in place." He was tempted to call additional members of the tactical team to help scope the place out. "I need to know what we're dealing with."

"That shouldn't be a problem." She hesitated, then added, "But I'd really like to check on Bailey first."

"We can." He could understand her need to see the little girl. "Although if she's napping, we may want to head straight there. She won't miss you if she's asleep."

"You're right." She blew out a breath. "I'm being foolish. There's no reason to rush back to the hotel. We may as well stop at the music hall now while we're out and about."

"If you're sure," he said, eyeing her thoughtfully.

"Yes. It makes sense to do that now." She shook her head. "You must think I'm an emotional wreck."

"Nope. I think you're a concerned mother," he said. "And I can appreciate your desire to see Bailey for yourself."

"Thank you, Zeke." She took his hand, and he could feel the diamond ring on her finger. "I really owe you big time for helping me through this."

"I'm more than willing to do my part," he said. "But at some point you'll need to run this past your lawyer. Maybe there are other ways to prove your ex isn't fit to share custody of your daughter."

"I already have my attorney working on it," she said.

"That's how I know Josh has an alibi that proves he wasn't anywhere near me when the first few notes were delivered."

"Maybe the police then?" he asked.

"Tried that too." She looked incredibly frustrated. "According to the detective I spoke with, the LA Police Department is up to their eyeballs in real crime. He also told me the notes aren't threatening enough to rise to the level of a stalker."

He could accept the part about the LA cops being up to their necks in real crime, but the notes absolutely fell into stalker-like activity. The vague threats were creepy.

Surprising that the LAPD hadn't taken them seriously. He supposed that despite her new career as a Christian solo artist, Sienna wasn't famous enough to force the issue.

None of that mattered now anyway, as the LAPD couldn't do anything about events that had happened here in Milwaukee.

"I don't like the fact that we don't have the recent notes on record," he said. They still had the brick in an evidence bag, though, and it was still on the floor between Sienna's feet. "I'd like to ask my boss, Rhy, to keep track of these events and to process the evidence without making a formal report."

She considered that for a long moment. "I guess we can do that, but I really don't want the information to leak out to the media."

"I hear you. We'll keep everything under wraps for as long as possible." He couldn't guarantee complete anonymity, especially if they ended up in another situation where a gunman opened fire on them.

He decided to make a quick detour to the precinct. Better to hand off the brick now than wait for another incident. He wasn't hopeful they'd lift any prints, but stranger things had happened.

"This isn't the way to the Sinatra Music Center," Sienna protested.

"We'll get there soon." He pointed to the brick. "After we drop that off." As he spoke, they passed the billboard announcing her show: *Sienna!* Along with a picture of her singing. The dates and times of her shows were listed, along with the venue.

Information publicly available to anyone who wanted to do her harm.

Yeah, they definitely needed to check out the Sinatra Music Center.

He found a parking space at the front of the precinct. After grabbing the evidence bag with the brick, he slid out from behind the wheel. He escorted Sienna inside, glancing around in confusion when he noticed the place was mostly empty.

The lab was open, so he dropped the brick and note off, then poked his head into Rhy's office. His boss was gone, as was Joe Kingsley, their second-in-command.

Only their tech guru, Gabe Melrose, was in his usual cubicle.

"What's going on?" Zeke asked.

"They're searching for an escaped behavior health patient," Gabe explained. "Guess the guy hears voices and has already killed one person having somehow gotten a hold of a knife. He escaped from one of the local hospitals. Not Trinity Medical Center, but a different one." Gabe smiled at Sienna. "Hi. I'm Gabe."

"Sienna Reynolds. Nice to meet you." Sienna returned his smile. "It's great to meet the people Zeke works with."

"Oh, yes. Uh, sorry, I should have introduced you." Zeke

belatedly realized he wasn't acting like a newly engaged man. "Gabe, this is my fiancée, Sienna. Sienna, this is Gabe, the tech expert for our team. We couldn't do our jobs without him."

"You're engaged! Wow, congrats!" Gabe accepted the news at face value. "I didn't even know you were seeing anyone."

"Don't blame him, I asked Zeke to keep things quiet until now," Sienna said. "Zeke and I grew up together in Greenland. In fact, he was my older brother's closest friend." She glanced around the mostly empty precinct. "I was so looking forward to meeting the others too."

"Maybe you can stop by again," Gabe said. Then he joked, "The way the team is getting engaged and married at the speed of light is a little worrisome for those of us who are still single."

"Yeah, getting engaged and married seems to be contagious," Zeke said with a smile. "We need to go. If you see Rhy or Joe, let them know I'll be in touch later, likely from a strange phone number."

"Why a different phone?" Gabe looked concerned. "Don't tell me the two of you are in danger too?"

"We're fine, really," Sienna said. "Just taking some extra precautions."

Gabe didn't look as if he was buying that, so Zeke gave him a warning look to butt out. "See you later, Gabe."

"It was nice meeting you," Sienna added.

Zeke led the way back to the main entrance. As they headed outside, Sienna glanced over at him.

"I don't know if any of your teammates would be interested, but I can probably get a bunch of complimentary tickets to the Sunday show. Friday and Saturday nights are already sold out, but Sunday has seats available."

"They would love to attend if they're able," he said. "A few of them have kids, so they might need to arrange for a babysitter. And most of them are believers too."

"Great." She looked pleased. "I'm so glad to hear that. And providing free tickets is the least I can do."

"Well, don't call your manager or anyone about that yet," he cautioned. "Not until we have the phone situation sorted out."

"Oh." Some of the pleasure faded from her eyes. "I almost forgot. I'll wait until we're about to leave the Sinatra Music Center to send a quick text. Dirk will be happy to make the arrangements."

He wanted to argue, but using her phone at the venue was probably okay. Especially since she'd be spending plenty of time there this upcoming weekend.

Maybe he needed to meet with this Dirk guy face-to-face. Were there others involved too? Like a PR team?

He decided to add meeting those closest to her to the lists of tasks that needed to be completed prior to the first show. For now, he wanted to see what they were up against with the layout of the venue.

"You have to pay for parking on the street." Her look was apologetic. "But this shouldn't take too long."

"It's fine. I think there's an app for that now." In truth, he didn't pay for parking very often because he was usually in a patrol car. As he circled the building looking for parking, he realized it was bigger than he'd anticipated. "How many seats does this theater hold?"

"Not that many, maybe twelve hundred or so?" She sat forward. "There's a spot."

"I see it." Twelve hundred people. His blood ran cold just thinking about that many people watching him do anything, much less sing. "Better you than me," he muttered half under his breath.

"Thankfully, I don't get stage fright anymore," Sienna said. "The Christian crowd is so much nicer than most. I feel blessed to share my talent with them."

"That's amazing." She had come a long way from doing plays at high school. He pushed out of the rental SUV and then used his phone app to pay the parking fee.

"This way." Sienna took him around to the back of the building. "There's a key code to get inside. I insisted on being able to hold my rehearsals here."

A horrible thought hit. "Do you have a whole band? People playing instruments? Backup singers?"

"No, I play a little piano or guitar as needed." She unlocked the door and stepped inside.

He was ashamed to admit he hadn't seen her perform since high school. And even then, he'd only gone because Luke asked him to. The back door led to a series of dressing rooms. Remembering her large suitcase, he had to smile. Compared to others, he was sure Sienna had packed light.

From there, they moved along the back of the stage amid lights and curtains. "Who manages these?"

"The stage crew." When he groaned, she added, "They work for the theater, not me. I highly doubt we have to worry about them. They've seen far more famous performers."

"Yeah, sure." The more he saw, the less he liked the setup. At this rate, he'd need the entire tactical team to have the theater surrounded, and it would still be impossible to protect Sienna.

Yet he doubted the goal was to kill her. A murder would draw an intense investigation, one that almost always led to the people closest to her. Or those with an axe to grind. He didn't think that Josh wanted to be in the crosshairs of an investigation, but he did want joint custody of their daughter.

He walked out on stage, scanning the rows of empty seats. Then he spotted the upper level. Easy to imagine Jina up there with her sniper rifle to keep an eye on things.

"Can we head up there?" He gestured to the location where he assumed lighting guys and other experts would be stationed during the show. "What's it called?"

"Here they refer to it as the front catwalk. But I'm not sure how to get up there. Hang on." Sienna crossed the stage, then ducked behind the curtain.

The stage was empty now, but he could easily imagine her standing there, singing her heart out.

"Zeke? Over here," Sienna called.

He turned and headed toward her as a crack of gunfire rang out. He dove forward, tucking and rolling across the stage. The shooter had to be up in the front catwalk.

And the gunshot had missed him by less than an inch.

CHAPTER FOUR

"Zeke!" Sienna had dropped to the stage floor, then began crawling toward him, her ears ringing from the crack of gunfire. The acoustics in the theater were such that noises were amplified. "Are you hurt?"

"Stay back!" His sharp tone made her freeze. Then he quickly closed the gap between them, both taking refuge behind the long black curtain. "I'm fine. But the gunman is up in the front catwalk!"

"How did he get up there?" The door to the theater had been locked. Sure, the stagehands knew the code, but how could anyone working with Josh have uncovered that information so quickly?

"I don't know. Stay behind me," Zeke instructed as he rose to his feet. "We're going to find a way up there."

"Okay." She swallowed the urge to run away without looking back. But that was impossible. She was under contract to perform. Gripping the back of Zeke's shirt, she stayed close behind him as he made his way through the curtained area.

There was a loud clatter from the other side of the stage.

Zeke swung around so fast she lost her grip on his shirt. She gaped when she saw he held a gun in his hand. He quickly but gently pushed her behind him before moving toward the other side. Upon hearing the pounding footsteps, he quickened his pace.

The sound of a door slamming shut made her think the shooter had left the building. But Zeke continued moving forward, peering carefully around the curtains as he traversed the stage. It occurred to her that he wasn't taking anything for granted.

Especially if there was more than one person involved.

Clearing the stage took time, and when they reached the door, she could see it hadn't closed all the way. Zeke pushed it open and glanced around. Then he pulled the door shut and turned to face her. "Let's take the stairs to check out the upper level."

"Okay." This probably wasn't the time to tell him she was afraid of heights. Swallowing her fear, she stayed close as he approached the metal stairs. Soon they were up in the rafters of the theater. She felt okay as long as she didn't look down.

"The shooter must have come this way," Zeke muttered. "He took advantage of me heading off on the opposite side of the stage."

She glanced that way, then quickly averted her gaze. "I'll take your word for it."

Zeke walked along the side of the rafter to the front catwalk. The area was wider up there, with two seats for whoever was manning the lights. A hint of vertigo hit when she saw how far down below the stage was located.

Don't look! Don't look!

"We can try to get crime scene techs up here," Zeke was saying. "The shooter may have left fingerprints behind."

"Uh-huh." She couldn't seem to force words past her tight throat.

"Are you okay?" Zeke peered at her, as if noticing her fear. "You should have told me you don't like heights. Hold on to me as we head back down."

She made another sound that hopefully sounded like agreement. She alternated between watching her feet and Zeke, without looking at the stage below, as they made their way back down.

"Okay, I think he's gone," Zeke said. "I need to check the stage. That bullet ended up somewhere."

A wave of dread washed over her. Obviously, they should call the police. Zeke was a cop, but this latest threat was serious. Especially as he was the one targeted this time.

Yet she knew that a shooting within the theater would roll through the news outlets faster than wildfire.

What should she do? Was it wrong to avoid getting these incidents on record? It seemed as if the shooter was amping up his attacks to force her into doing just that.

Lord Jesus, guide me! Show me the way!

The prayer brought a bit of peace. Until she saw how methodically Zeke was walking the stage, searching for evidence.

Of a bullet!

She didn't know how things had spiraled so far out of control. One minute she was dealing with threatening notes, the next dodging bullets.

"I don't know what to do." She hadn't realized she'd spoken the words out loud until Zeke glanced at her.

"We're going to talk to my boss about these recent events, while keeping them off the record for now." He came over to stand beside her. "But we really need to think through our next steps. The shooter is escalating. Two attempts in a few hours is not good. And he could easily make another attempt against you during one of your shows."

"Except you're the one he fired at this time. Not me." A shudder rippled over her. "I don't think you should keep protecting me. Maybe I can hire some other bodyguard. Someone . . ." She couldn't finish the thought.

"No, Sienna. I'm staying. Besides, I know you well enough to understand you won't take anyone being hurt on your behalf lightly. Not even a total stranger." He wrapped his arm around her shoulders, giving her a brotherly hug. "I'm fine. And I honestly don't think this guy would have killed me."

She wasn't convinced. "Maybe Josh thinks that getting you out of the way will help his case against me."

"Josh doesn't even know I'm involved," Zeke said. "And the cold-blooded murder of a cop would bring the entire police force raining down on the bad guys. However, you make a good point. Josh will know about me as soon as we announce our engagement." He scanned the stage. "I don't see the bullet, but everything behind the stage is black, which makes it hard to identify the path of the bullet."

He kept talking about the shooting as if it was an everyday occurrence. Then again, for him, it probably was. She hadn't considered that asking for Zeke's help would put him in harm's way. The notes had been threatening but otherwise harmless.

Gunfire was not.

"I don't know what to do," she repeated. "If we go to the police, the word will get out about the threats. It may even scare people off from coming to the show. If we don't, this guy may keep trying." If she canceled her contract, she doubted anyone would ever take another chance on her.

She was still new in the Christian music scene and needed to keep the momentum going.

And really, how else could she support herself and Bailey? God had granted her this gift of singing. She didn't have many other skills.

"Hey, don't worry. We're going to get to the bottom of this," Zeke said, his expression reassuring. "Don't give up hope. Let's head back to the precinct. Maybe Rhy or Joe have another idea."

"Okay. Should I still call Dirk?" She was so badly rattled she couldn't remember why she'd planned on calling him in the first place.

"I was thinking you should announce our engagement during the morning show interview," Zeke said. "And you don't have to worry about the tickets."

Oh yes, that was it. She had planned to tell Dirk about the engagement and get complimentary tickets. "I . . . guess I could do that. It would give me something to talk about other than my singing career." Truthfully, she wasn't looking forward to the morning show interview, but public appearances were part of the deal.

Especially when she needed to convince the public to come out to see her.

"Let's get out of here." Zeke drew her toward the rear door. Then he abruptly stopped to look at her. "Who's your contact for the theater? We need to get the entry code changed."

"Those arrangements went through Dirk." She took her phone from her pocket and took a moment to power it up.

"Don't tell him about the gunfire," Zeke warned. "Just mention that some stranger accessed the building, and you want the code changed."

"I can do that." She did her best to sound calm when Dirk answered her call.

"Sienna, where have you been? I've left several messages." Dirk sounded upset.

"Sorry about that." She evaded the question. "I'm here at the music venue, and some stranger got inside. I need you to contact the tour company to let them know I need the access code changed ASAP."

Dirk sighed. "Okay, fine. I'll make the call. But you can't be too demanding, Sienna. I need you to come across as easy to work with."

"I am easy to work with, but as a single mother, safety will always be a concern. I'm sure the tour company will understand as long as you frame it properly."

"Yeah, yeah. Fine. But there are other interview requests coming in. Did you listen to my messages?"

"Not yet, but I will. I wanted you to also know that I'm engaged to be married."

"Engaged?" He sounded shocked. "Who's the lucky guy?"

"Zeke Hawthorne, a very close friend of mine. I'll announce my engagement during the TV interview. I'll be in touch later, Dirk. Bye." Without giving him a chance to respond, she ended the call and quickly powered down the phone.

"I'm not sure we can trust him," Zeke said with a frown. "He's coming across very demanding, almost as if he resents you going off-grid."

"He probably does resent it, but he'll get over it." She didn't know what to think about Dirk or anyone else associated with this tour.

Zeke was the only man she could trust.

THE SHOOTER SHOWING up at the theater was concerning, and frankly, Zeke wasn't sure what to do about it. He was more than willing to act as Sienna's bodyguard, but having Flynn as backup wouldn't be enough.

At this point, he wasn't sure that having the entire team surrounding Sienna and Bailey would be enough.

Plus, he wasn't sure how long they'd be able to keep the news of these attempts against her under wraps.

The main problem was that they'd been playing defense since last night. Reacting to the note, the brick through the window, and the two recent shooting attempts. Other than getting their replacement phones, a computer, and his mother's engagement ring for Sienna, he hadn't made any headway on the case.

Specifically digging up dirt on Josh Allenton.

"Stay back for a moment." He tucked Sienna behind him to peer out the back door. Sweeping his gaze over the people milling about and the cars driving back and forth, he didn't see anyone suspicious.

Not that he'd recognize the shooter if he saw him.

Spying a group of college students coming down the street in their direction, he decided to use them as cover. "Let's go." He reached for Sienna's hand and quickly escorted her to the car. The students barely glanced at them as they walked by.

Less than a minute later, they were on the road heading toward the precinct. Using his phone, he called Gabe. "Have either Rhy or Joe come back yet?"

"They're five minutes out. Sounds like Cassidy found our escaped perp." Zeke picked up on the hint of pride in Gabe's voice. Their tech guru had a not-so-secret crush on

Cassidy Sommer. "Do you want me to tell Rhy you're on the way?"

"Yes. We'll be there in ten." Zeke was glad to hear the tactical team had come through again. Over the past few years, they'd made several significant arrests. Still, Rhy was always under pressure from Assistant Chief Michaels to rein in their budget. "Gabe, I may need your help to dig in to a guy by the name of Josh Allenton. It's complicated because he's a current resident of California, in the LA area."

Gabe whistled. "Sounds like a challenge. If Rhy's okay with it, I'm happy to see what I can come up with."

"I'll talk to Rhy. I'm sure he'll go along with the plan." At least, he hoped so. He glanced at Sienna. "Do you have Josh's phone number?"

"Yes, I have it memorized." Without hesitation, she rattled off the ten digits. The area code was that of Milwaukee, which surprised him.

"Why does Josh have a Wisconsin number?"

"He grew up here too. Up in Green Bay, but we met here in Milwaukee at the university. We were in the same choir group." She shrugged. "Neither of us was really keen on getting a four-year degree in business or communications. Our blended voices garnered us a fair amount of attention. We decided to head to LA where we sang at various clubs. From there . . ." Her voice trailed off, and it took her a minute to continue. "Well, you know the rest. We ended up getting married. Less than two years later, our relationship slid downhill."

"I see. I'm sorry to bring up a painful subject, but it's important for me to know these things. I didn't realize Josh would know his way around the city."

"Yes, but I'm telling you, he's not here," she repeated

stubbornly. "He's in LA where he'll bend over backward to make sure at least a dozen people can vouch for his whereabouts during the time frame of the shooting."

"But that doesn't mean he didn't find someone else here in Milwaukee to do his dirty work," he said calmly. "Maybe even someone he went to school with."

Her jaw dropped. "You think so?"

"Yep." The more he considered the possibility, the more he warmed to the idea. "I'll need the names of Josh's known associates from back then. His college roommate, the guys he hung out with."

She blew out a breath. "I'll try, but that was a long time ago."

"Your life and Bailey's depend on that information." He didn't want to scare her more than she already was, but he needed those names. "It wouldn't be easy for anyone from LA, for example, to find their way around the city. And vice versa."

"I'll make a list." She sounded more confident now. "I remember his college roommate was Brett Voss. I don't know if Brett and Josh stayed in touch, though."

"It's a place to start." He was thrilled to be able to give Gabe another name to work with. "Keep thinking back to those early days of your relationship," he encouraged. "Maybe something else will come to you."

"I know his old girlfriend was Analise. Analise Waverly." She shrugged. "They were dating when we first started out. "

"Oh yeah? And how did it end?" he asked.

"Josh broke things off. I remember Analise wasn't happy about it; she accused me of stealing her man." Her expression turned grim. "She should consider herself fortunate to have escaped him."

"Maybe you'll get a chance to tell her that." Analise was another person of interest to investigate. His earlier despair had been replaced with a cautious confidence.

Today was Tuesday. They had three days before Sienna would be standing on that stage performing in front of a crowd of strangers.

Three days to find the shooter and get the evidence needed to convict Josh of hiring a stalker to get custody of his daughter.

Sure, he thought sourly, *piece of cake.*

He pulled into the parking lot located along the side of the precinct. He covered Sienna as best he could, making a mental note to pick up more body armor while they were there.

At the rate things were going, he'd need it.

Too bad he couldn't cover Sienna in Kevlar from head to toe while she performed. Or better yet, put up a bullet-resistant plate of glass to separate her from the rest of the crowd.

As they entered the building, he was glad to see Rhy stood near one of the desks talking to Joe. He took Sienna's hand the way he would if they were truly engaged and headed toward them.

"Rhy, Joe, I'd like you to meet my fiancée, Sienna Reynolds." Zeke hoped he looked like a happy groom to be. "Sienna, these are my bosses, Captain Rhy Finnegan and Lieutenant Joe Kingsley."

"It's a pleasure to meet you both," Sienna said, her voice smooth as silk. "Zeke has told me so much about you."

"Funny, we haven't heard nearly as much about you," Rhy drawled as he shook her hand.

"Yeah, congrats," Joe said, when it was his turn to reciprocate.

"Oh, please don't be angry with him. It's my fault that Zeke has kept our relationship secret." Sienna's smile faded a bit. "I asked him to wait to say anything until all the details for my opening tour were set. I, uh, plan to announce the exciting news during my Thursday morning interview on the Milwaukee Morning show."

"Is that so?" Rhy's skeptical brown eyes latched onto his.

"Yes, it's true." He lifted their clasped hands. "I gave Sienna my mother's engagement ring. She would be thrilled to know that Sienna and I have rekindled our love. Sorry to have kept you both in the dark."

"Does this mean you're leaving the team?" Joe asked.

"Oh no, absolutely not," Sienna said, before he could respond. "Zeke and I both love the area. You know we grew up in Greenland, right?" Her laugh sounded genuine. "I've always had a crush on Zeke, and it turns out he felt the same way. It's thrilling to know that we'll start our new life together right here where it all began."

Again, Rhy's piercing gaze bored into his. He held his ground, hopefully hiding his true thoughts. He knew he could trust Rhy and Joe with the truth, but it seemed easier to go along with the engagement story.

At least, for now. He honestly wasn't sure how long he could continue evading the truth, though. Having a fake engagement was a lot more difficult than he'd anticipated.

After a long moment, Rhy nodded. "That's wonderful news, then. Congrats on your upcoming wedding."

"Yes, absolutely," Joe agreed. "When's the big day?"

"Oh, ah, we're waiting until Sienna has finished her tour." He wished he'd taken more time to look at her schedule for future shows. He had no idea how long her tour was for.

"Yes, I finish up in Hot Springs, Arkansas, with a Christmas program." Sienna tightened her fingers around his. "We're thinking maybe early next year."

"Oh, wait! You're that Sienna?" Joe's expression lit up with recognition. "My wife, Elly, and I have been listening to your songs! Absolutely amazing."

"That's so sweet, thank you." Sienna blushed, as if she wasn't accustomed to hearing praise. "The glory goes to God, though, right? I have complimentary tickets to the show on Sunday if anyone is interested."

"I am," Joe said, raising his hand. "We'll find a babysitter."

"We are too," Rhy echoed. "I know Devon would love to attend. Although, we'll also need to find a sitter."

Zeke wasn't surprised the guys from work were jumping on the chance to see Sienna's show. "I'll make sure everyone gets tickets," he said. "But in the meantime, we could use a little help. Sienna's ex-husband is causing some trouble. And we can't go through the usual channels to get answers."

Instantly, Rhy's and Joe's expressions hardened. "What's going on?" Rhy asked.

"Please don't let this information get out into the media," Sienna said, still clinging to his hand. "I would like to keep this quiet unless there's absolutely no other option."

Joe and Rhy exchanged a look. "Fine with me," Joe said. "Fill us in so we know what we're up against."

Zeke was humbled by how quickly Joe and Rhy jumped on board. It made him feel a little guilty for lying about their engagement. He did his best to push the regret aside. "The guy in question is Josh Allenton. He's currently residing in LA but grew up in Wisconsin the same way we did. Sienna filed for divorce after he physically abused her, and she was granted sole custody of their daughter, Bailey."

"Josh is now fighting for co-custody," Sienna said. "And I think he's behind several attacks on me. If he can convince the judge that some stalker is after me and Bailey would be safer with him, then I'll lose the custody case. And that cannot happen. Josh doesn't really care about Bailey or anyone but himself. He's only doing this to hurt me." There was a brief pause, before she added, "And it's working. I'm worried sick over this."

"Okay, first thing we need is to have Gabe begin digging into your ex-husband's background," Rhy said. "I doubt you're the first woman he's abused. If we can find others, that will help solidify your case against him."

"I actually asked Gabe to do that on our way here." Zeke quickly filled them in on the various threatening notes along with the most recent shooting incidents. "Part of the problem is that Allenton comes from money. We believe he's hired someone else to do his dirty work. I would like to think this guy he hired is just trying to scare us, but the gunfire at the Sinatra Music Center was a little too close for comfort."

"Don't suppose we can change the venue?" Joe asked.

"No, I'm under contract, and the first two shows are already sold out," Sienna said.

"The good news is that her first show is Friday night, so we have a couple of days to find this guy," Zeke said. "If we can get him into custody, I'm sure we can convince him to cooperate. He'll face significant charges unless he tells us who hired him."

"Yeah, I can see how that could work. But we could use more intel to go on," Rhy said.

"I have a few more names to give Gabe," he said. "And once we're settled in the City Central Hotel, we'll try to come up with additional leads."

"Who's watching your daughter now?" Joe asked, his gaze full of concern.

"Flynn agreed to come out to stay at the hotel with Bailey and my live-in nanny, Taylor," Sienna said. "I truly can't thank each of you enough for helping me through this. I—well, I obviously made a mistake in marrying Josh. The minute Zeke and I reconnected I realized how I never truly loved Josh. Marrying him was the worst decision of my life." Her blue eyes reflected her sorrow. "But God graced me with the gift of a beautiful child. I can't bear the thought of my daughter suffering because of my mistake."

"Bailey is going to be fine," Zeke hastened to reassure her. "Flynn won't let anyone hurt her. Or your nanny."

"Maybe we should check the nanny out too," Rhy said.

"I did a quick background check, and she is a professional nanny, but I agree that Gabe should work his magic on Taylor Templeton," Zeke said. Then he frowned at Rhy. "I hope you don't get in trouble over this. We don't have an official case file to show for Gabe's time, and I know Michaels is always asking you to watch the budget."

"Don't worry about that." Rhy waved off his concern. "We may eventually have to submit a case file, but for now, we'll keep Gabe's work on this under wraps."

"Thank you very much." Sienna's voice was low and husky with emotion. "Zeke told me you wouldn't hesitate to help. I appreciate your support more than I can say."

"Hey, you're marrying this guy." Rhy slapped him on the back. "That makes you family. And in here, family trumps everything."

"Yep," Joe agreed. "We've got your back."

"Thanks, guys." Zeke smiled through his guilt. "I'll get these names to Gabe, then we'll head back to the hotel."

"I'll let Gabe know he can work on this for the rest of the day," Rhy said.

Zeke nodded, then turned toward Sienna. Before he could lead the way to Gabe's cubicle, she stepped into his arms and brushed a light kiss across his lips. "I love your family, Zeke."

For the life of him, he couldn't find his voice. In some remote part of his mind, he assumed Sienna was playing the role of his doting fiancée, sealing the deal for Rhy and Joe's benefit.

But the potency of her kiss had fried his brain cells.

Making him wonder what it would be like if their engagement was for real.

CHAPTER FIVE

Oh boy. Sienna should not have given in to the impulse to kiss Zeke. If she were completely honest, she'd admit she had done it more from curiosity than playing up their fake engagement.

But she had seriously underestimated the impact of his kiss. Fleeting as it was, she'd felt the sizzle of awareness all the way down to her toes.

"Ah, we should get to the hotel, right?" She forced a cheerfulness she didn't feel into her tone.

"Yes. Of course." Zeke seemed flustered too. She really shouldn't have kissed him. He took her hand and led her through the precinct to the rear entrance.

Glancing over her shoulder, she noticed both Rhy and Joe were watching. She gave them a little wave, making a mental note to make sure Dirk arranged for the comped tickets.

"Uh, Zeke? I need to call Dirk about the complimentary tickets to Sunday's show." She tugged on his hand to stop him. "You don't want me to use my phone in the hotel, so I should do that here."

"Yeah, good idea." He nodded and released her hand. "If you can get extras, we'll offer them to the rest of the team too."

"Absolutely." Giving Zeke's teammates complimentary tickets was the least she could do. She was touched by how his bosses rallied around them, anxious to help out in every way.

A far different experience from the report she'd filed in LA. To be fair, she hadn't known any of those officers on a first-name basis.

Still, shouldn't most cops want to help a woman in trouble? Especially a single mom with a two-year-old daughter?

Hearing Dirk's grumpy voice in her ear pulled her back to the issue at hand. "One more thing," she said, talking over his complaint that she'd ended their earlier conversation so abruptly. "I need twenty comped tickets for Sunday's show."

"Twenty? For who?" Dirk demanded.

"Friends of mine." She was becoming irritated herself. "Why do you care? The show isn't sold out. Twenty tickets together in a group, not individual seats spread out around the theater, understand? Thanks, Dirk." Again, she quickly ended the call before he could draw out another argument.

"I don't like your manager," Zeke said. "He sounds like a jerk."

Dirk the jerk had a nice ring to it, but she managed to keep it to herself. "Dirk isn't a bad guy, he's just a little high-strung. This is a huge opportunity for me, and I think he's concerned I'm going to ruin it."

"It's your career, not his." Zeke scowled. "He should be more concerned about supporting you."

"To be fair, his career is pretty much tied to mine." She powered off her phone. "I'm his biggest client to date and that has made him extra nervous. I'm sure he'll relax a bit once these first few shows are finished."

Zeke looked as if he might say something more but didn't. Instead, he led the way to the rental SUV. Seeing it reminded her of the need to reimburse him for the daily fees. Once they were back at the hotel, she'd make a list.

After a moment, she noticed Zeke headed north rather than southeast toward the hotel. Turning in her seat, she scanned the cars behind them. "Do you see something suspicious?"

"No, but that's the point." He glanced at her. "I need to be absolutely sure we're not followed to the City Central Hotel."

"I understand." And she appreciated his diligence. It was tempting to call and talk to Flynn again, even though she knew Zeke's friend would let them know if anything was amiss.

A wave of exhaustion hit hard. They'd left the hotel intending to run a couple of harmless errands, only to end up being shot at twice. The near miss inside the Sinatra Music Center was the most troubling.

She would be performing on that stage in three days. Even with Zeke's team surrounding the stage, she'd be vulnerable to an attack.

If killing her was the objective.

Thankfully, she didn't really think that was the shooter's intent.

She turned her attention to the scenery outside the car. The fall colors were nearing their peak, the stunning red, orange, and yellow leaves fluttering in the wind. This was the reason she'd wanted to start her tour in her hometown. While living in LA, she had missed experiencing the four seasons.

Even winter, despite the cold. Snow could be as beautiful as the colors decorating the trees.

"I, uh, still need you to think about who Josh knew when you were both attending the university here," Zeke said, breaking the silence.

Kissing him had made things awkward between them. "I'll try. I just wish I had paid more attention back then."

"Well, it's not like you could have expected things to turn out like this," Zeke said.

"True. I really made a mess of my life."

"Don't think of it like that." Zeke took her hand. Suddenly the previous awkwardness was gone. This was the man she knew and cared for. Best to keep their relationship on a friendship basis. "God has put you on this path for a reason. I'm sure you wouldn't be a Christian musician if not for the breakdown of your marriage."

"You're right about that. And I have been blessed with a beautiful daughter." Thinking of Bailey caused tears to prick her eyes. She would do whatever was necessary to provide a safe home for the little girl. And if that meant sinking in every dime she made doing this tour to pay for the legal fees, then so be it.

"We're going to get through this," Zeke murmured. "You don't know Gabe Melrose, but he's exceptional at his job. We have his support along with the rest of the team. I know the others will chip in to help too."

"I know. And I'm thankful." She cupped her hands around his. "Thank you, Zeke. I couldn't do this without you."

"Hey, that's what friends are for." His tone was light, but the intense look from his dark-brown eyes indicated he was serious. He turned to the left, finally taking them back toward the lakefront.

Who had Josh been friends with? She'd given Zeke the names of his roommate Brett Voss and his old girlfriend, Analise Waverly. But there had been another guy Josh had talked about. What was his name? Her fingers itched to turn on her phone to check Josh's social media pages.

If he still had them up and active. Her social media was managed by Dirk's PR team. The posts were mostly about her tour and snippets of videos from her live shows.

She wasn't keen on having her personal life included and had flat-out refused to feature any pictures or posts about Bailey. Still, she couldn't control everything. Images of her and Bailey were likely out there in the cyber world.

Just the thought of Josh following her on social media made her feel sick to her stomach. She knew that her recent and somewhat unexpected success within the Christian world gnawed at him. He blamed her for the demise of their short career, and for their subsequent divorce.

Without taking any responsibility for the physical abuse he'd subjected her to.

"Ken Holt," she said, the name popping into her mind. "Kenneth Holt was another one of Josh's friends."

"Great work," Zeke said with a smile. "What do you remember about him?"

"Nothing good." She sighed. "Ken thought he was hot stuff and hit on me several times, telling me I could do better than Josh. Which in hindsight, was true. But I was annoyed he seemed to think I would cheat on Josh. Especially since Ken always seemed to have a new girl in his life."

"We'll see if we can uncover more information about him." Zeke sounded confident. "It's nice to have several possible suspects."

"Analise Waverly, Brett Voss, and Ken Holt." She found

it difficult to imagine any one of them hiding in the front catwalk and taking shots at them. Well, maybe Ken Holt would do something like that. There was always something rather sleazy about him. "We should start with Ken."

"Sounds good." Zeke continued to watch the rearview mirror as they headed back to the hotel. Even though she trusted Flynn and Taylor, she was anxious to see Bailey.

"I'm going to park around back," Zeke said as the building came into view. "We've used that area in the past. There's a rear door we can use to access the building."

"Works for me." Her stomach rumbled loudly with hunger, making her flush with embarrassment. Their errands had ended up taking all morning. "Oops. Sorry about that."

"We'll order room service for lunch," Zeke said with a smile. "I'm hungry too."

After parking in the back, Zeke came around to open her door for her. Then he grabbed their bag of disposable phones and the new laptop computer.

The area was completely deserted as he used the hotel key to access the door. Inside the hotel, she quickened her pace to reach their suite.

"Hold on, I want to warn Flynn." Zeke used the phone to call his buddy, who then opened the door.

"Hey, you guys were gone longer than we expected," Flynn said. "I had to convince Taylor not to call and check on you."

"Yeah, well, I have a few things to fill you in about." Zeke closed and locked the door.

"Mama." Bailey toddled toward her, lifting her arms up. Heart melting, Sienna bent and swept the little girl into her arms.

"I'm here, sweetie." She buried her face against her

baby's sweet hair. The moment reinforced what really mattered.

Nothing was more important than her daughter.

ZEKE'S HEART squeezed at the poignant way Sienna held Bailey close. She was a wonderful mother and a phenomenal singer.

It burned to know her ex-husband was trying to take it all away from her.

He caught Flynn's curious look and nodded. His buddy needed to know about the recent shooting attempts. And that Rhy and Joe had approved of their using Gabe as a resource to help them track down those responsible.

"We were just thinking about ordering lunch," Taylor said.

"Great idea." He strode toward the table to grab the menu. "We'll eat first, then talk strategy."

Flynn arched a brow, clearly anxious to know more. The menu wasn't extensive, but he wasn't picky either. "I'll go with the basic cheeseburger. Sienna? What would you like?"

"I'll try the chicken ranch wrap. Let's try some of the chicken strips for Bailey too."

"Great." A few minutes later, Zeke had placed their lunch order. Then he worked on activating their new disposable phones.

"You got a computer too?" Flynn asked.

"We need all the help we can get." When Sienna took Bailey into the other room to change her, he added, "A shooter showed up at the music center. We need to identify this guy, ASAP."

Flynn whistled. "Not good."

"Tell me about it. Changing the venue is out of the question, and the clock is ticking. We have three days to find this guy. Thankfully, Rhy is on board with Gabe helping us."

"Where do we start?" Flynn asked.

It was a good question. "I think we should keep Gabe focused on digging into Sienna's ex-husband. We have a few names of known associates that we can start looking into."

"Okay, I'm in." Flynn shook his head. "But if this guy has money, he can hire anyone."

"I've considered that." Zeke prayed they weren't heading down the wrong path. Time was not on their side. "But Josh has been in LA for a while. I was hoping he'd have gone to his former Wisconsin friends for this job."

"That's an excellent theory." Flynn rubbed his hands together. "What do you need from me?"

Zeke had to smile. "You take Brett Voss, Allenton's former college roommate. I'll focus on his sleazy friend Kenneth Holt. There's also a former girlfriend in the picture, but we can put her on the back burner for a while."

"I'm not sure about that," Sienna said, returning to the room. She set Bailey on the floor. The little girl walked straight toward the dolls Taylor had sitting on the floor beside her. "A woman scorned can be just as vindictive as a guy."

"But if Josh dumped her for you, why would she help him out?" Zeke asked.

"Maybe he's repaired his relationship with her." Sienna shrugged. "I don't know who Josh is dating these days, but I guarantee he's not spending his time alone. He's got someone new in his life by now, which will only reinforce his image of being a changed man." Her voice held a hint of bitterness.

He couldn't blame her for being upset and angry. The guy who'd promised to love her had betrayed her in the worst way possible, striking at her in anger, then seeking revenge by trying to get custody of their daughter. Why the jerk didn't just accept reality and move on with his life was a mystery.

"Okay, that's another place to start." Zeke wished he had connections within the Los Angelos Police Department. Maybe Rhy could reach out to someone higher up in the food chain. He sent Rhy a quick text, then turned back to the computer. Rhy responded with an okay sign, indicating he'd give it a try.

"We should look at Josh's social media," Sienna suggested, leaning over his shoulder to see the screen. "See if he's still on those sites."

It didn't take long. "I found him. Looks like he hasn't been very active in the past year, though," Zeke admitted as he clicked through various photos. "I don't see him with a woman either."

"May I try?" Sienna nudged him aside. With a few keystrokes, she had signed in as her professional profile and was back on Josh's page. It soon became clear he hadn't blocked her from his accounts. It didn't take long for her to sigh. "He's taken a huge chunk of old photos down. I think he's whitewashed these accounts to improve his image."

That explained why he hadn't blocked her. There was nothing important there for her to find. "It's okay, we'll keep looking. Could be that some of those photos are still up on other people's sites. We'll keep at it."

"You're right. He'll have made a mistake somewhere along the way." Her smile didn't quite reach her eyes.

They worked until their food arrived. After saying grace, Sienna took on the task of feeding her daughter between taking bites of her wrap so that Taylor could eat uninterrupted. Not for the first time, he wondered why a young woman like Taylor would take a job like this. One that required her to live with a single woman and a child. Sure, maybe the pay was good, but not having any time to herself seemed like a significant sacrifice.

He caught Flynn's gaze, giving a subtle nod in Taylor's direction. His buddy shrugged and kept eating. The layout of the suite made it difficult to have a confidential conversation about the nanny.

But then Flynn snagged the computer closest to him and began to work while munching the last of his fries. A message popped up on his phone.

I'm on it.

Zeke hid a smile and typed back. *Thanks.*

Bailey started to fuss before Sienna had finished eating. "I can take her," Taylor offered.

"No thanks, I'll do it." Sienna used a napkin to wipe Bailey's hands and face. "You had her all morning. It's my turn. Come on, sweetie. I think you're tired. It may be time for another nap." Sienna lifted the little girl up and carried her to the closest bedroom.

"I know what you guys are thinking," Taylor said the moment Sienna was gone. "It's obvious you don't trust me. I can't change that, but you need to know I'd never allow anything to happen to that baby."

"Never said you would," Zeke drawled. "Sienna has been the target of these threats, not Bailey."

Taylor frowned. "I wouldn't hurt Sienna either."

"You have to admit, this is a pretty sweet gig," Flynn

drawled. "Food and board, along with part-time work. Not bad."

Taylor flushed. "You're cops, so I'm going to let that slide, even though I'm not the bad guy here."

"No offense, but we don't know that. We don't know you either," Zeke felt compelled to point out.

Taylor muttered something unkind under her breath. "Fine. What do you want to know? Maybe this is a different career choice than what you guys are used to. It's not a crime. I like being a nanny. I enjoy taking care of Bailey and working for Sienna. She pays me a decent salary and always chips in to help with Bailey unlike some of the rich people I've worked for in the past." She rose to her feet, her expression stern. "Whatever you think of my job, just know I'm not involved in this."

Zeke had to admit that Taylor sounded sincere. Maybe they were passing judgment on her career choice, but he wasn't going to apologize for considering her a possible suspect. She didn't understand that this was how all cops operated.

And her simply saying she was innocent wasn't good enough.

"We're not saying you would hurt anyone," Flynn said, voicing his thoughts. "But you can't blame us for double-checking your story." He glanced up from the computer to pin her with a pointed glance. "You grew up in Madison as the oldest of three kids?"

"I don't believe this," she muttered. "You already know the answer to that, so why ask me? Yes, I grew up in Madison. Yes, I did a lot of looking after my younger siblings while both our parents worked. It seemed natural for me to pursue a degree in early childhood education. I may decide to go into teaching, which was my original goal."

"What made you change your mind?" Zeke asked, truly curious now.

"I was a nanny for a lawyer over the summer, and I enjoyed the work. They didn't need me during the school year but referred me to another family. The Sterns offered me a live-in nanny position, so I figured I'd give it a try. I didn't mind the work, but the Sterns were nothing like the Johnsons. In fact, they couldn't have been more opposite. They treated me like a servant. I was expected to do the dishes, the laundry, and clean the house in addition to taking care of their two children. That wasn't bad, but they constantly criticized me because things weren't clean enough for them. Even a few toys scattered about earned a frown. This from parents who completely ignored their own children when they were home." She paused to take a breath, then added in a calmer voice, "I stayed with the Sterns for a year before moving on. Last I heard, they've gone through four nannies since then. I lasted the longest."

"Sienna said your references were stellar," Zeke said to smooth things over. "And I know she trusts you."

She nodded and began stacking their dirty dishes together. Flynn jumped to his feet. "I'll take care of that. You go do—um—whatever you do in your free time."

Taylor threw up her hands. "I write, okay? If you must know I'm writing a book, a romance. One that will not include a hero that is anything like either of you!" She turned away, flopping down onto the sofa.

"Ouch," Zeke murmured. "You sure stepped into that one."

Flynn shrugged and continued stacking dishes onto the tray. "Better she takes her anger out on us."

"Hey, check this out." Zeke had stumbled across a

photograph of Brett Voss standing beside Josh Allenton. "Looks like our target has kept in touch with his old college roommate after all."

Flynn leaned over to see the picture more closely. "Interesting. I wonder where Brett Voss is now?"

"Give me a minute, there's an age listed on his profile." Zeke couldn't help but grin. "Nice of him to include the month and date of his birth. We know he's roughly Josh's same age, too, so that helps narrow it down." Zeke typed the information into the DMV database. "Bingo. I found him. He still has a Wisconsin driver's license."

"That's great." Flynn slapped him on the back. "See if he has a vehicle registered to his name."

"He does . . . but it's a blue Chevy Blazer." He thought back to the car that came up behind them. "Not the same make and model as the guy who fired at us earlier today."

"Could be a rental. Especially if Mr. Megabucks is paying the bill." Flynn winced, glancing over to where Taylor was curled up in the corner of the sofa. "I guess I should keep the rich jokes to a minimum."

"You think?" Zeke shook his head. "I'm with you on the rental, though. If nothing else, Allenton would want to cover his tracks. He wouldn't want anything obvious leading back to him."

"Okay, you're on the right track," Flynn said. "Let's keep at it. We're bound to uncover more connections to this guy, and one of them will lead us to the shooter."

"I'm very concerned he was inside the theater," Zeke said in a low tone. "I keep thinking this guy is getting information from someone close to Sienna."

"You could be right. Although from what I'm seeing, it's no secret Sienna is scheduled to perform this upcoming weekend. It probably isn't that hard to get inside the place either." Flynn went back to stacking the dishes. "Give me a minute to set this tray in the hallway, then we'll divide and conquer."

"Yeah, okay." Zeke rose to his feet and stretched. He glanced toward the bedroom where he could hear Sienna singing softly to Bailey. He was too far away to hear the words, but the cadence of her voice was soothing.

Taylor noticed, too, her gaze softening. "That's why I like working for Sienna," she said.

Flynn braced the tray on one hand as he opened the door. He set it down, but then said, "Hey, who are you?"

Remembering how a hotel employee shot through the door a few months ago in an attempt to kill Roscoe and his pregnant girlfriend, Libby, Zeke darted toward the sofa to drag Taylor out of the way. He practically pushed her toward the closest bedroom door as the sound of gunfire erupted from behind him.

"Go," he shouted as he reached for his weapon. Then he turned to back up Flynn.

"He's getting away!" Blood dripped down Flynn's arm, but the wound didn't look serious. Beyond Flynn's shoulder he saw a man dressed in black sprinting down the hall.

"Stay with the women!" Zeke took off after the perp. Unfortunately, the gunman was taking advantage of his head start. The guy dressed in black plowed through the rear exit and disappeared.

Zeke followed, but when he reached the door, he could see the guy was already halfway down the street, meshing with the other pedestrians heading to and from the court-house. A split second later, he lost sight of him completely.

Frustrated, he turned back to join Flynn. Letting the

guy go wasn't easy, but Flynn was injured, and they needed to move.

There wasn't a moment to waste. Nothing was more important than keeping Sienna and Bailey safe.

CHAPTER SIX

Sienna had just gotten Bailey to sleep when she heard the gunfire and Zeke's shouting. Without wasting a moment, she grabbed the diaper bag and held Bailey close as she ducked into the bathroom.

Heart racing, she hid behind the door. Where was Taylor?

Please Lord, keep us all safe in Your care!

She should have let Taylor put Bailey down for her nap. After this, she wouldn't blame Taylor for giving her notice. As it was, Taylor wasn't keen on traveling for the next three months. The lure of moving around seemed to be wearing off.

At the rate these attacks were coming, Sienna worried she may be forced to cancel her tour altogether.

Swallowing hard, she did her best to soothe Bailey as she listened. Then she heard Zeke calling her name.

"Sienna? Sienna, are you okay?" He opened the bathroom door, his dark eyes filling with relief when he saw her and Bailey. "You're not hurt?" When she shook her head, he nodded. "Good. We need to get out of here."

"And go where?" She couldn't imagine they'd be any safer in another hotel. Although clearly staying here wasn't an option. She resisted the urge to throw herself into Zeke's arms. "I don't understand what happened."

"I don't either. Get your stuff together. I'm hoping we can use the safe house." Zeke already had his phone out and was turning away. "Rhy? We're in trouble. The gunman showed up and fired at Flynn."

Taking a steadying breath, she shifted Bailey in her arms and packed what she could in the diaper bag. Thankfully, there hadn't been time to unpack her large suitcase. As she worked, the fear she'd have to cancel her tour wouldn't leave her alone.

She had an obligation to uphold her contract, but at what cost?

Was this Josh's master plan? She'd assumed he wanted her to be in danger to get custody of Bailey, but maybe he also wanted her to give up the income from her shows.

Paying a lawyer would be difficult if she had to refund the advance she'd been given.

Pushing those thoughts aside for the moment, she pulled her suitcase with one hand while still carrying Bailey. She froze when she found Taylor inspecting Flynn's bleeding arm.

"What happened?" Releasing the oversized suitcase, she rushed forward. Zeke hadn't mentioned anyone had been hurt. "You were hit?"

"It's nothing," Flynn said. "Just a flesh wound."

"Sienna, hand me the diaper bag, would you?" Taylor sounded amazingly calm. "I need the cleaning wipes and bandages."

"Of course." She shrugged the diaper bag off her shoulder and handed it to Taylor. As Taylor rummaged for what she needed, Sienna glanced over at Zeke who finally ended his call with Rhy.

"We have the safe house for the rest of the week. Flynn, we'll need to pile into your car. It will be tight, but I'm concerned the rental is compromised."

"That works." Flynn dug the key fob from his pocket and tossed it at Zeke. Then he frowned at how Taylor was gently cleaning the wound on his upper arm. "Hurry up and slap a bandage on that so we can hit the road."

"Okay." Taylor quickly did as he asked, then stood and slipped the diaper bag over her shoulder. "I'm ready."

Zeke grabbed her oversized suitcase, carrying his weapon in one hand as he moved toward the door. "Sienna, you and Bailey stay close to me. Flynn, grab the car seat and the computers if you can. It's not going to be a quick getaway, so I need everyone to be on high alert for anyone who looks remotely suspicious."

"I can grab the phones." Swallowing hard, she snagged the bag of disposable phones as she followed Zeke out to the front of the hotel where Flynn's vehicle was located. There were several cars in the parking lot, which she felt certain must be a good thing. The shooter couldn't know which one belonged to Flynn. Zeke gestured to a nice-sized SUV, but with four adults and a bulky car seat, he was right about it being a tight fit.

By unspoken agreement, she and Taylor squished into the back seat once she'd secured Bailey in the car seat. Taylor tucked the diaper bag at her feet so they could access it if needed. Zeke tossed her large suitcase into the back, then he took the driver's seat. Flynn grumbled as he slid into the passenger seat.

"That didn't take too long," Sienna said as Zeke merged into traffic.

Zeke met her gaze briefly in the rearview mirror, then turned his attention to the road. "Flynn, did you get a good look at the guy?"

"White guy, about my height with brown hair." Flynn scowled. "He wasn't wearing a ski mask, but I had to duck when he fired at me. I was going to return fire, but by then, he turned to run."

Sienna felt sick at how close Flynn had come to being badly hurt, or even dying. This situation had spiraled out of control. She could not in good conscience ask Zeke and Flynn to continue putting themselves in harm's way for her and Bailey.

But what was the alternative? She refused to give Josh custody of their daughter. She could flee the country. Maybe go to South Africa or Australia. Find a way to buy a couple of fake names for her and Bailey. A drastic step that would make her a fugitive from the law. Yet right now that seemed the smarter path to take.

For Zeke's and Flynn's sake. And really, for anyone with the misfortune of being near her and Bailey.

A cloak of despair settled over her shoulders as she tried to smile and softly sing to her daughter. Bailey was making it known she hadn't gotten her nap, but soon the soothing car ride lulled the little girl to sleep.

"It's going to be okay," Taylor whispered. "Zeke and Flynn will keep us safe."

"I know." What Taylor said was true, but it was also the crux of her dilemma. This running from threats and gunfire was wearing her down. She had not anticipated Josh would go to these lengths to get to her.

She wanted to pepper Zeke with questions about how the gunman had found them and what they were going to do next but held back so as not to wake Bailey.

Everyone was silent as Zeke navigated the streets. She noticed he eyed the rearview mirror several times along the way, making sure they weren't followed.

She hadn't used her phone in the hotel, so how had the gunman found them? By tracking Zeke's rental car? That seemed like a stretch, but then again, if Josh had access to unlimited funds, maybe he'd hired a former cop to find her.

"Does Josh know about our friendship?" Zeke's voice was a whisper.

She shook her head. "I didn't talk about you to him. I don't know if Luke ever mentioned your name, but I doubt it. Luke didn't care for Josh."

Zeke nodded without saying anything more.

After nearly twenty minutes of driving, Zeke turned into what appeared to be a residential neighborhood. Flynn turned in his seat to look back at them. "You'll like the safe house," he said in a whisper. "There are three bedrooms and a kitchen. And the windows are all made of bullet-resistant glass."

"Sounds good." She tried to smile, but the fact that they were at the point of needing a safe house with bullet-resistant windows was hardly reassuring. Sure, they'd be safe unless they wanted to walk out the door.

Zeke pulled into the driveway but kept the engine running in an effort to keep Bailey asleep. He pushed open his door and jumped out.

Flynn did, too, and soon the two guys had all their belongings inside the safe house. She gently eased Bailey from her car seat and carried her inside.

She went into the closest bedroom and put her daughter on the bed. Then she placed pillows around the little girl so she wouldn't roll off. Keeping the door open an inch so she could hear her if she awoke, Sienna returned to the living room.

"Rhy? We're set." Zeke was back on the phone. "We could use a replacement vehicle, though, just to be extra cautious." Zeke met her gaze, then added, "I have to assume this guy found us by tracking the rental. I parked it in the back of the City Central Hotel, and that's the same door he used to access the building."

She sank into the closest chair, thinking back over their morning. The shooter had left the theater before they had, was it possible he'd been sitting somewhere nearby and had seen which car they'd gotten into?

Was this guy really that good?

Although he hadn't hit what he was aiming at, so maybe he was better at finding them than at hitting his target.

She shivered, despite the warmth of the room. First Zeke had nearly been hit by gunfire, then Flynn.

It was only a matter of time before the gunman would turn his sights on her. Or worse, her daughter.

Now that they were safe, she needed an exit plan. A way to disappear, forever.

***

ZEKE COULD TELL Sienna was distraught over their most recent tussle with the gunman. He didn't blame her and wished he'd asked Rhy about the safe house from the beginning.

Then again, he was fairly certain the gunman had gotten a line on the rental while they were at the Sinatra Music Center. Maybe it was better that they were able to escape the hotel while leaving the rental car behind.

He really needed to do a better job at keeping Sienna and Bailey safe. Thankfully, Flynn's injury wasn't serious.

But the gunman had still gotten far too close.

"Would you like me to look at your arm again?" Taylor asked Flynn.

"Nope. I'm good." Flynn shrugged off her concern.

"I'm so sorry this happened," Sienna said. "I feel terrible you were injured because of me."

"Not your fault," Zeke quickly said. "Don't worry, we'll find this guy. The description Flynn gave resembles Josh's roommate Brett Voss."

Sienna stared down at her clasped hands for a long moment before meeting his gaze. "It might be time for a new plan. One that involves me and Bailey obtaining new identities and disappearing for good."

What? He stared at her in shock. "You can't do that, Sienna."

"Why not?" She spread her hands. "This isn't working. I can't ask you and Flynn to put your lives on the line just so I can sing."

"For one thing, you'll be in trouble with the law if you don't show up in court to fight against your ex-husband's request for custody." She obviously didn't understand what was at stake. "Every cop across the country will be looking for you and Bailey."

"I have sole custody now," Sienna said. "The next court hearing is a month away. Plenty of time for the two of us to disappear."

He didn't point out that he and Flynn were both obligated to uphold the law. Even if he wanted to skirt the legal issues, he'd never ask Flynn to do the same.

He took two long steps, then he knelt in front of Sienna, taking her hands in his. His mother's engagement ring winked up at him, giving him strength. "We have three days until you're scheduled to kick off your first show. A day and a half before you're scheduled to do the morning show interview." Time was slipping by faster than he cared for, but he continued to hold her gaze. "I'm asking you to be patient. To give us a little time to work on this. Don't forget, we have the tactical team backing us up."

"I don't know what to do," Sienna said in a low, anguished voice. "It feels selfish to keep moving forward."

"The gunman has broken the law," he reminded her. "He is the one being selfish. Along with the guy who hired him."

She stared at him for a long moment. "I guess I can give you a few days. But if I have to cancel, it would be better for everyone if I at least gave those ticket holders some advance notice. At least twenty-four hours."

"I'll see what we can do," he rashly promised. Two days would be pushing it. Unless Gabe was able to find something on Josh Allenton that would help turn the tables in their favor. "I think we're on to something with Brett Voss who is likely living in this area. And we still need to dig deeper into Ken Holt."

Sienna's fingers tightened around his for a moment, then she nodded. "Okay. Two days. If we're not farther along in identifying the gunman, I'll cancel the show."

While she didn't add anything about leaving under a fake name, he understood that was still her backup plan. One that he could not morally or legally get on board with.

But that was a problem for another day.

"Thanks." He released her hands and rose to his feet. Flynn was in the process of setting up the two computers in the kitchen. With the sound of a ticking clock echoing in his mind, Zeke quickly joined him. "Let's pick up where we left off with Voss."

"Yep." Flynn had already brought up Brett Voss's photo. After studying it for a long moment, he grimaced. "I don't know, Zeke. This might not be the guy I saw. The perp's eyes were closer together, and his nose wasn't as prominent."

Like all cops, Flynn had a keen eye for detail. The information was depressing, but he wasn't ready to give up on Voss yet. "Maybe Voss has a buddy. Let's keep searching. Oh, and we should probably follow up with Gabe soon."

"I realize we just ate lunch, but we'll have to think about food at some point," Flynn said.

"I'll check the cupboards," Sienna said, coming into the kitchen. "Maybe the former residents have left some food items behind."

Zeke watched Sienna as she moved through the kitchen, then forced himself to look away. This was not the time to think about how attractive she was. Or how much he liked and admired her.

Not when he only had two days to find this jerk.

He reached for his phone, hesitated, then opened the bag containing the disposable phones. After pulling one out, he dialed Gabe's number.

"Who is this?" Gabe asked in lieu of a greeting.

"Zeke and I'm here with Flynn. Please make a note of this number, we're going low profile from this point forward."

"Yeah, I heard you guys were found at the City Central Hotel," Gabe said. "Rhy and Joe have gone to smooth things over."

He knew Rhy would pull out all the favors he had to keep the shooting incident off the radar, but the hotel wasn't within their jurisdiction. Since there was nothing Zeke could do to help Rhy and Joe, he focused on Gabe. "Did you find anything we can use on Josh Allenton?"

"Nothing major. I uncovered a few underage drinking tickets, a disorderly conduct ticket, and a minor drug possession charge involving marijuana. Then, of course, there was the assault charges that Sienna filed against him." It seemed as if Gabe had been busy. "I did notice that he had the same lawyer representing him for each offense. Dude by the name of Walter Rowe."

"Walter Rowe," Zeke repeated, causing Sienna to turn and look at him.

"That's the Allenton family lawyer," Sienna said. "Rowe didn't represent him in our divorce, but he is the one Josh is using in his new joint custody request."

"Good work, Gabe. According to Sienna, Josh's lawyer is being paid for by his parents." He thought for a moment, half listening to Gabe's fingers clacking on the keyboard. "Is Rowe only licensed to practice in California? Or can he practice here in Wisconsin too?"

"He's licensed in three states: California, New York, and Wisconsin," Gabe said. "Why, is that significant?"

"I don't know, probably not." He wondered how the attorney had become so loyal to the Allenton family. "Although I would like you to keep digging into the family. Maybe this is just how rich people operate, but it seems strange to have a lawyer willing to drop everything on a dime."

"More like a quarter, or even a dollar," Gabe said.

"What?" He wasn't following.

"The phrase 'drop everything on a dime' refers to the days when you could put a dime in a pay phone and make a call . . . never mind. Rhy's on the other line. Gotta go." Gabe abruptly ended the connection.

"I think it's fairly common for wealthy people to have lawyers on retainer," Sienna said. "At least, Josh has always had legal support to fall back on." Her brow furrowed. "Rowe called me directly after I had Josh arrested for assault and battery. He tried to convince me to drop the charges."

That shouldn't have surprised him, but it did. "I hope you told him off."

"I did. Thankfully, my lawyer had prepped me well." Her features relaxed. "From that day on, I refused to speak with Josh or his lawyer. I figured it was better to pay the legal bills than go through the stress and anxiety."

"How did they make their money again?" He eyed her curiously. "You mentioned Josh grew up in Green Bay. Unless he was a professional football player, I don't think that area boasts many millionaires."

"No, it wasn't football." She frowned. "I believe Josh's dad was one of the founders of a tech start-up business. Something related to microchips. Maybe it was the newest version of them, I can't say for sure. All I know is that his dad's business took off at warp speed."

"And when was that exactly?" he asked.

"I think that was after our sophomore year. I was twenty, but Josh had just turned twenty-one." She grimaced. "We were young and foolish really. But I remember Josh mentioning how his parents wanted him to transfer to Stanford University because they were moving to LA, which was ridiculous as his grades were awful. Not nearly good enough to be accepted to Stanford, even if that was what Josh wanted."

"And that's when you began to sing?" he pressed.

"Yes." She looked down at the floor, then sighed. "I can't lie, the lure of moving to LA was difficult to resist. We decided we'd give it a year or two to see if we could launch our singing career."

He understood what she didn't say. That Josh's parents had supported them financially during those early years. He didn't blame her for wanting something better. Although he wondered what her brother, Luke, had thought about that.

A subject for later. For now, he needed to stay focused on Josh and his family. There was nothing suspicious about a tech company growing like gangbusters. Or the desire to move to LA. Silicon Valley was home to the big tech giants. He could see why the move to California may have been helpful. "I appreciate you sharing that information."

She opened her mouth to say something, but Bailey's wail prevented her from speaking. "I'll get her," Taylor called.

Sienna turned away, leaning against the kitchen counter for a moment. Flynn shot him an arched look, so he stood and crossed over to her. "Are you okay?"

"Fine." The word was clipped. "Just wishing I'd been smarter back then."

"You're plenty smart. You were young and wanted to believe the best in people." He hesitated, then added, "And I doubt Josh revealed his true colors until you decided you had enough and managed to escape."

"Yes, that's true." Her smile was sad. "Josh did not expect me to fight back. I think he figured his money would be enough to keep me." Her blue eyes darkened. "He was wrong. I don't care about the money, other than what I need to fight his attempt to get custody of Bailey."

He wanted to offer her his financial support, but cops didn't make a high salary. Although he had inherited his mother's house free and clear, along with her engagement ring. "I can mortgage my house if needed. We'll figure something out so you don't have to disappear with Bailey."

She held his gaze for a moment, then turned away. "I'm not taking your money, Zeke. This is my problem. I'll figure it out."

"We're in this together." He caught her hand and tugged her to face him. "We're engaged, remember?"

She jerked her hand from his and began wiggling the ring off her finger.

"Don't, please?" He glanced over his shoulder to where Flynn was still working. "You gave me two days. Let's keep things as they are for now."

She sighed and nodded, sliding the ring back onto her finger. Then to his horror, a tear rolled down her cheek.

"Sienna." He pulled her into his arms, hugging her much like he had when he'd attended her brother's funeral. Totally platonic, despite their brief yet heated kiss. "We're going to get through this. You need to have faith in God's plan."

"I'm trying." Her voice was muffled against his shirt.

He drew her from the kitchen and into the living room to give her some privacy. "I know this has been hard. But I promise we're safe here."

"It's not that. It's everything." She lifted her watery gaze to his. "I hate Josh for doing this. We're supposed to forgive those who hurt us, but I can't, Zeke. I don't know how to forgive Josh for this."

"You don't have to," he said, even though he knew from attending church with some of his teammates that she was right about what the Bible said. "You don't have to forgive him yet. To be fair, we don't know that he's the one behind this."

"Oh, he is responsible." Anger flashed in her eyes. He preferred seeing the anger over tears. "Who else would do this?"

"I agree, it's suspicious. But you don't know for sure this isn't the work of some deranged fan. Someone who has become obsessed with you." He tucked a strand of her dark hair behind her ear. "You're a beautiful woman with the voice of an angel. I don't think we can discount an obsessed superfan just yet."

"I wish this was the work of a not totally sane superfan, but you know as well as I do that these attacks are personal." A reluctant smile tugged at the corner of her mouth. "But I appreciate the kind words."

"I only speak the truth." Despite his efforts to treat her like Luke's sister, his gaze dropped to her mouth. The urge to kiss her was strong enough to have him leaning toward her. And even better, she held his gaze without pulling away.

"Hey, Zeke?" Flynn's excited voice crashed the moment. "I think I have a line on our second perp, Josh's old buddy Ken Holt. He looks more like our shooter, although I couldn't swear to it in court."

"Coming." No point in wishing for something he couldn't have. Their engagement wasn't real.

Worse, if he didn't figure out who their shooter was and soon, Sienna and Bailey were likely to disappear from his life forever.

CHAPTER SEVEN

What was she thinking? Kissing Zeke was asking for trouble. Sienna didn't need to add another complication to her life.

She liked and trusted Zeke. Cared about him. But the last thing she wanted was to get involved with another man. Even one as handsome, sweet, honorable, and protective as Zeke Hawthorne.

Oh boy. Just the fact that there was much to admire about him spelled trouble. She didn't have time for this. Her entire future was in limbo. She'd given Zeke two days to make progress on identifying the shooter before she took matters into her own hands.

Granted, she wasn't sure how to go about getting fake IDs for herself and Bailey. A basic ID may not be hard, but a fake passport to get out of the country would take skill and money. Probably lots of money.

Would she really circumvent the legal system like this? Just to keep her daughter safe?

Yes. In a heartbeat.

"Sienna? What do you think?" Zeke's voice penetrated her troubling thoughts. Realizing she was still standing in the living room, she moved to the kitchen table. Zeke stood and gestured for her to take his seat. "This is a recent photo of Ken Holt."

Seeing Josh's sketchy friend made her shiver. She turned to glance up at Zeke. "Is this a mug shot?"

"Yep. He did time for selling drugs, but he's out of jail now." Zeke's brown eyes narrowed as he pulled out his phone. "I'll call Rhy to have a BOLO issued for this guy."

"But we don't know that he did anything illegal," she protested.

"We can pick him up as a person of interest," Flynn said. "Considering he has a rap sheet, we have the right to question him."

That made sense. This was Zeke's area of expertise, not hers.

"Rhy? We have a suspect we'd like to interview." She listened as Zeke gave Rhy the pertinent details on Ken Holt. "We're requesting a BOLO for Holt and his car, a silver Toyota Camry." He rattled off a license plate number. "And I'd like someone from the team to head out to his apartment. See if he's there."

His apartment? Hope flared in her heart. Maybe Zeke and his teammate would find the shooter, and she wouldn't be forced to go into hiding.

"Thanks, Rhy. Keep me updated." Zeke lowered the phone. "Cassidy and Jina are heading to Holt's last-known address."

"I'm surprised you were able to access so much information," she said.

"We're good," Flynn teased. Then his expression turned serious as he tapped an index finger on Ken's mug shot filling the computer screen. "Do you remember seeing him hanging around recently?"

"No. And I was cautious, especially after I received the first threatening note." She stared at Ken's face. She'd never liked Josh's friends back when they were first together. The years had not been kind to Ken; he looked like a hardened criminal. The blank stare reflected in his eyes made her shiver.

"Okay, just thought I'd ask." Flynn turned the computer so he could keep working.

"How quickly will he get picked up?" she asked. "If he's not at his apartment, I mean."

"Depends." Zeke shrugged. "If your ex has hired him to go after you, I'm sure he's doing his best to hide from anyone remotely resembling a cop. And we know he's using a different vehicle, as we haven't seen the silver Camry."

It was depressing, but she tried not to show her despair. "Well, I hope the police find him."

"We will. And we'll keep digging," Zeke said. "Being in the safe house is great because it's one less thing for me to worry about."

"I understand." Leaving the guys to it, she stood and moved down the hall to find Taylor and Bailey. Bailey was up from her nap, and the two were sitting on the floor playing with toys Taylor had pulled from the diaper bag.

For a moment, she simply watched her daughter with a heavy heart. It wasn't right that Josh should make things difficult for a two-year-old. If he cared about Bailey, he wouldn't create a situation where his daughter was in danger.

Then again, she'd learned the hard way that Josh didn't care about anyone but himself.

She sat on the floor to join the fun, but her mind kept

going back to Ken Holt and the possibility of Josh hiring him to shoot at her. And at Zeke. Did Ken realize Zeke was a cop?

Would it matter? It should, but thinking of Ken's cold eyes, maybe not.

"Mama." Bailey climbed into her lap. "Fishes?"

Bailey loved cheesy fish crackers. "Sure thing."

"Why don't you let me change her first," Taylor offered. "Then I'll bring her into the kitchen for a snack."

"Thanks, Taylor. I'll see what we can do about dinner." She'd only started going through the cupboards and had found a half dozen cans of soup, a box of crackers, a handful of spices, and very little else. Whoever had stayed here previously hadn't done much cooking. Or maybe they hadn't had to spend much time here.

A reminder they wouldn't be here for long either.

She headed back to the kitchen and opened the fridge. There were several bottles of water and diet soda, but nothing else. The freezer contained three frozen pepperoni pizzas and a tray of ice cubes.

Bailey liked pizza, and she figured the guys wouldn't mind the simple fare either. She turned to ask when they wanted to eat when Zeke's phone rang.

"Hawthorne," Zeke answered, clearly not recognizing the number. Then his gaze lifted to hers. "Hey, Cass, thanks for calling. You're sure Holt doesn't live in that apartment any longer?" He listened for a minute, then sighed. "Yeah, okay, I understand. See if you can get the manager to call you back with a forwarding address. Thanks."

"No sign of Ken?" she asked when he pocketed the disposable phone.

"Nope. Allegedly, Holt moved out three weeks ago." He frowned. "When did you get the first threatening note?"

She had to think about that for a minute. "About ten days ago. Why?"

"Your show has been advertised for several weeks now," Zeke said. "I'm trying to figure out when Allenton put his master plan in motion."

"Josh filed for joint custody three weeks ago." The time frame clicked in her brain. She could easily imagine Josh reaching out to Ken Holt, offering him a bunch of money for the job of stalking her. She tried to focus on the issue at hand. "It takes weeks to get court hearings on the docket, and I remember thinking Josh chose the date to file on purpose to interfere with my upcoming tour."

"Allenton filed for joint custody at about the same time Holt moved out of his apartment." Zeke glanced at Flynn. "They know each other, but there isn't any proof that Holt is the shooter."

"We need someone to see the BOLO and pick him up," Flynn agreed. "I'll keep poking into his social media, maybe I'll spot a photograph of him in a local hangout. People tend to keep going back to the places they're familiar with."

"That's true." Zeke's dark eyes gleamed with anticipation. "Holt isn't a professional, so it's likely he's made some mistakes."

"But if Ken isn't a professional, how was he able to track your SUV and the rental as well?" she asked.

"Resources," Zeke said. "Money can buy resources. I'm sure Josh has paid someone to access the DMV database to get a line on my vehicle. The rental could have been identified while we were outside the Sinatra Music Center."

She nodded, but the Ken she knew wasn't that savvy. Then again, Ken had done time in jail and could have learned a few tricks of the trade. "You said Ken was arrested for selling drugs?"

"Crack cocaine," Zeke said. "According to the police report, they caught him selling the stuff but in small quantities. Hence his short stint behind bars."

"I see." She had to take his word for it since she didn't really understand how the legal system worked. In many cases, it seemed as if many criminals got off rather easy.

If they did time at all.

But that wasn't her problem. She took heart in the possibility of finding Ken Holt, who would hopefully turn on Josh to save himself.

They needed to prove Josh was the one behind these attacks. Attempted murder and/or murder for hire were serious charges. She had to believe Josh would end up in jail once this was over.

And if not, she and Bailey would disappear. Forever.

* * *

ZEKE COULD READ Sienna like a book; her expressive face reflected her thoughts. She was hopeful they'd find Ken, yet he knew she was also resigned to carrying out her threat to take Bailey out of the country.

He decided not to point out how difficult that would be. He'd rather spend the next two days finding Ken Holt and/or Brett Voss.

Zeke never understood the lure of gambling, but he'd bet his paycheck that Josh had hired one of his former friends to do his dirty work. Sticking around in LA with a new girlfriend to establish an alibi was his attempt to ensure he wasn't considered a suspect.

"May I ask one of you to get Bailey's car seat?" Taylor asked. "Bailey wants a snack, and we don't have a high chair."

"Sure. I'll grab it." Flynn jumped up from the seat. "Zeke, toss me the keys."

He did, then turned his attention back to Holt's social media posts. The guy didn't post often, and so far Zeke hadn't stumbled across any pictures of a restaurant, a bar, or a gym.

Holt had to hang out somewhere.

Just then he stumbled across a picture of Holt standing near a wooden railing wearing a T-shirt. Zooming in on the screen, he examined the shirt's logo.

The Wooden Nickel.

A quick search revealed the Wooden Nickel was a bar down on the north east side of the city. The location wasn't too far from the neighborhood where his teammate Raelyn and her husband, Isaiah Washington, now lived. The crime rate there wasn't low, and he had to give Raelyn and Isaiah credit for trying to change the neighborhood.

He sent a quick text to Raelyn asking for intel on the Wooden Nickel as Flynn returned with the car seat. Moving the computer off to the side, they were able to prop the car seat in a chair and push it close to the table in a makeshift high chair.

"Thanks," Taylor murmured as she dumped several cheesy fish crackers on the table. Bailey grabbed several, shoving them into her mouth. "No, sweetie, one at a time, remember? We only eat one at a time."

Bailey grinned, cheese smeared on her face. She picked up a fish cracker with each hand, showing them to him as if intending to share. "One, two, free!"

He couldn't help but smile as she shoved both crackers into her mouth. Bailey was adorable, and watching her only made him that much more determined to find Josh's accomplices, putting an end to the attacks once and for all.

The Wooden Nickel was a place to start.

He leaned forward to grab Flynn's attention. "I need to leave for a short while to check this place out. Will you keep an eye on things here?"

"I can stay here, but I don't think you should go alone," Flynn said with a frown. "Take Cass or one of the others with you."

"Go where?" Sienna asked.

"Have you heard of a bar called the Wooden Nickel?" He turned the screen to show her the logo on Ken Holt's shirt. "It may be nothing, but I'm going to head over to take a look."

"I'm coming with you," Sienna said. "If Ken is there, I might be able to convince him to give up Josh."

"I can do that." Zeke tried not to show his irritation. "I'm a cop, you're not. Remember what happened at the music center?"

"Exactly why I'm going with you." She tilted her chin stubbornly. "I'm serious about this, Zeke."

So was he, but he squelched a retort. A text came in on his phone, and he was glad to see Raelyn had responded. *WN is ok, meet you there?*

He texted back. *Yes 20 mins.*

K. See U then.

He caught Flynn's gaze. "Raelyn isn't far from the Wooden Nickel; she'll meet me there."

"Who is Raelyn? And why is she meeting us there?" Sienna asked.

"Raelyn is another member of the team, she lives with her husband, Isaiah, and their adopted son, Leon." He gave Sienna a stern look. "There's no reason for you to tag along. You're safer here."

"Please, Zeke. I really want to help." It was difficult to

resist her pleading gaze. "Maybe I'll see someone else there that I recognize from the old days. I'm at the center of this mess." She glanced briefly at her daughter, then added, "Don't shut me out."

He tried to come up with an argument that would convince her to stay back but couldn't. Maybe she had a point about recognizing others who might be involved.

Or maybe he couldn't find the willpower to deny Sienna the chance to get out of the safe house for a little while. He couldn't deny feeling a bit caged in himself.

"Okay, but you need to promise to do as I say." He ignored Flynn's knowing smirk. "If anything looks off, you'll have to wait in the car."

"Whatever you say," she agreed. "But I seem to remember Ken Holt had other friends he hung around with. It was almost ten years ago, but I'm hoping I'll recognize them when I see them."

"Fine." It was a good point. Besides, they'd already wasted too much time arguing. "Let's hit the road."

"Thank you." Sienna turned to Taylor and Flynn. "There are three pepperoni pizzas in the freezer. If Bailey gets hungry, go ahead and feed her first. We'll eat when we get back."

"Sounds good. Be safe, Sienna. You too, Zeke." Taylor's gaze held concern. While he hadn't found anything suspicious in the nanny's background, he couldn't decide if she was legit or a really good actress.

For Sienna's sake, he prayed Taylor wasn't involved.

He headed to the door, clicking the key fob to unlock the car they'd left in the driveway. He made a mental note to park in the garage when they returned.

"Where is this place?" Sienna asked.

"Not far from the River West neighborhood." That was

a section of the city that developers were working to revive. Unfortunately, its location adjacent to the crime-ridden north side of the city made that difficult. He eyed the setting sun, knowing they had less than two hours of daylight left.

It was always better to avoid the north side after dark.

Knowing Raelyn was meeting them there eased some of his concern. The three female cops on the team might all look like runway models, but they were tough and could hold their own even in hand-to-hand combat.

Especially, Jina. She was lethal.

"I really appreciate you letting me come along," Sienna said.

He arched a brow. "You didn't exactly give me a choice."

She frowned. "You don't understand what it's like. I can't just sit back and pretend Josh isn't trying to ruin my life. Using our daughter to get some sort of sick revenge on me."

"You're right, I don't know what it's like to be in your shoes," he admitted. "But you called me for help because I'm a cop. And I know what I'm doing."

"That's true. But the truth is, I just couldn't sit there doing nothing." She turned to stare out the passenger-side window for a moment. "It's strange how so much of the city looks unchanged, while other parts look completely different."

He lived there, so he couldn't say the same. The changes that had occurred over time were subtle enough that he couldn't remember what it was like before.

Another stark reminder that Sienna and Bailey didn't live there. They hadn't moved from LA to Milwaukee. For all he knew, she still had a place back in Los Angeles.

Sienna was only in town long enough to perform three shows.

The thought was a bit depressing. Yet he accepted that he and Sienna were destined to just be good friends. Being on tour, going from one singing gig to the next, was not the least bit appealing.

No, as soon as he found and arrested the gunman, he and Sienna would go their separate ways. His main goal now was to wrap this up within the next two days.

A little less than two days, he silently amended. The hours seemed to be going by too fast with nothing to show for their efforts.

All he could do was keep pushing forward, following every lead while praying God would grant him the strength and guidance he needed to protect Sienna and Bailey.

They drove in silence for a solid ten minutes when his disposable phone rang. He dug it from his pocket. Glancing at the screen, he quickly answered when he recognized Raelyn's number. "Hey, Rae."

"Zeke. I'm here at the Wooden Nickel. Are you still in transit?"

"Yeah, maybe five minutes out." He glanced at Sienna who was listening to his side of the conversation. "We were delayed leaving the safe house."

"Safe house? You better fill me in on what's going on," Raelyn said. "I was off work today, so I'm out of the loop."

"I'm here with Sienna, my . . . fiancée." He hoped Raelyn wouldn't pick up on his brief pause. "She's in danger, and we have reason to believe—"

"What? Engaged? Since when?" Raelyn interrupted. "You've been awfully flirty for being engaged."

He hid a wince when Sienna's eyes widened. Raelyn was speaking loud enough for the entire world to hear.

"Knock it off, Rae. I don't flirt. And I've known Sienna for years; we grew up together. Her older brother, Luke, was my closest friend. We even served in the army together. Just because I choose to keep my personal life private doesn't mean you should jump to conclusions."

"Look, I can buy that you were dating her, but engaged? Come on, Zeke." Her tone reeked of skepticism. "You have to admit that news came right out of left field."

Clearly, he'd never make it as an actor. He strove for patience. "I think the correct response here is congratulations, I'm so happy for you."

"Congratulations," Raelyn repeated. "And I am happy for you if this is for real."

"Thanks, we're thrilled. We're going to settle down in my mother's house in Greenland." That earned him another surprised look from Sienna, but he ignored it. He decided to keep playing the role of Sienna's fiancé for now, no matter how difficult. It wouldn't be long before Raelyn and the others on the tactical team would know the truth.

They'd be hurt about being lied to, but they'd get over it. Most of his teammates had been in difficult situations over the past year, and he knew they'd each gone out on a limb for the woman, or in Raelyn and Jina's case, the man they'd loved.

His engagement might be fake, but his feelings were real.

"Go on, what were you saying?" Raelyn's voice penetrated his thoughts. "Something about your fiancée being in danger?"

"Yes. We believe her ex-husband has hired someone to stalk her, to help sway the judge to grant co-custody despite his being charged with assault and battery."

Raelyn digested that for a long moment. "Okay, so who do you think will be at the Wooden Nickel?"

"One of her ex-husband's old friends, Ken Holt. There's also a former college roommate by the name of Brett Voss. We have issued a BOLO for Holt as he has a prior arrest for selling drugs."

"Okay, I'll see if I can pull up his info before you get here." Without saying anything more, Rae ended the call.

After pocketing the phone, he exited the interstate and headed east. He wasn't sure what to say about Raelyn's comments, so he kept silent.

"You have every right to flirt with other women," Sienna said in a low voice. "I feel bad for putting you in a situation where you have to lie to your friends."

"It's fine." Time to change the subject. "Check it out. That's the Wooden Nickel up ahead." The corner bar had a coin-shaped light in the window. He drove past the establishment first, taking note of Raelyn sitting in her SUV about a block down the road. He gave her a nod as he passed her, then went around the block. He pulled over to park on a street perpendicular to where Raelyn was.

He waited for Raelyn to slide out from the SUV before killing the engine. He glanced at Sienna. "Stay close and follow my lead."

With a nod, she pushed out of the passenger seat. Hoping this wasn't a giant mistake, like going to the music center, he climbed out of the car and reached for Sienna's hand. There wasn't much traffic, so they quickly crossed the street, approaching the bar from the front as Raelyn approached from the side.

Raelyn paused at the main entrance, waiting for them. He and Sienna quickly joined her. He double-checked to make sure his shirt covered his weapon, while Raelyn adjusted her fleece sweater to hide hers.

"Let's do this," he murmured, stepping forward to open the door. "Rae, you first. Sienna, stay behind her."

Raelyn took the lead, entering the dimly lit bar. It appeared to be a typical tavern, tacky beer signs hanging on the walls, and there was a poker machine sitting on the far corner of the bar.

The guy behind the bar eyed them suspiciously. Considering there were only two older men inside, Zeke couldn't understand why the bartender didn't look happy to have additional customers.

Then his gaze narrowed as he realized the bartender was Ken Holt. A bushy beard covered much of his lower face, and he wore a ball cap low on his forehead, but Zeke was convinced he was their guy.

Before he could warn Raelyn, Ken Holt ducked through a door behind him and disappeared. Seeing Sienna must have tipped him off.

"Cover the front," he shouted to Raelyn as he leaped over the bar to follow Holt. He quickly discovered the back door led down a narrow hall. Hugging one side to avoid being hit by a bullet, he pulled his weapon and moved forward.

"Police!" Zeke injected all the authority he could muster into his tone. "Ken Holt, you need to come out with your hands up where I can see them!"

For a long moment, he didn't hear anything. He moved a little faster now, hoping to catch Holt hiding out.

At the end of the hall was a door hanging ajar. Poking his head out, he scanned the area.

But saw nothing. Holt was gone.

CHAPTER EIGHT

Sienna saw the flash of recognition in the bartender's eyes a split second before he ducked through the door to get away from her. So much for her plan to convince him to talk.

Of course, Zeke vaulted the bar to follow him.

"Stay inside!" Raelyn darted out the main entrance without waiting for her to answer. She understood both Zeke and Raelyn wanted her out of the way.

"Who are you?" one of the two older men sitting at the end of the bar asked. He had white hair surrounding a bald spot that topped his head.

"Yeah, what's up?" his cohort added with a scowl. "How are we supposed to get another drink now that you've scared off our bartender?"

She pasted a smile on her face. "I'm sorry for your troubles. I'm sure your bartender Ken will be back soon." It was a blatant lie, and the two men knew it. If she had any money on her, she'd offer to pay for their drinks. But she didn't. Besides, since Ken had taken off, she felt certain these two wouldn't have to pay for the drinks they'd already downed.

"You someone famous?" the older white-haired guy asked, squinting at her. "You look familiar."

"No, I'm not famous." She suspected he may have seen the billboard sign her PR firm had sprung for, but there was no point in disclosing that after this. She eyed the bar with a frown, expecting Zeke to reappear at any moment.

"Must be a model." The younger of the two men smirked. "Bet she's in one of those girlie magazines."

"Nope. I would never do something like that." Where was Zeke? It wasn't that she couldn't handle these two old guys, but she was hoping Zeke would have returned by now with Ken Holt in custody.

"Make yourself useful and pour us another beer." The older guy held up his empty glass.

"I don't work here." She waved a hand at the empty bar. "Either help yourself or get out."

At that moment, Zeke emerged from the doorway behind the bar. The resigned expression in his eyes wasn't reassuring. "Is Raelyn out front?"

"Yes." She didn't have to ask if Ken got away; it was clear the bartender was gone. Zeke crossed over to where the two men sat.

"We're closed," Zeke said. "Time to move on."

The two men looked as if they might argue but must have decided to take advantage of the free drinks instead. They slid off their stools and stumbled to the doorway. Sienna moved out of the way, then followed them outside. Zeke spent a few minutes behind the bar, maybe locking things up for the owner, then joined her.

"He got away?" Raelyn asked.

"Yeah, I lost him." Zeke did not look happy. "I should have anticipated this and had you covering the back."

"It's my fault," Sienna said, guilt weighing heavily on her shoulders. She had insisted on coming along, only to have lost their best chance of bringing this nightmare to an end. "He bolted the second he recognized me."

"It's fine. I'll update the BOLO." Zeke turned and scanned the small parking lot. "I don't see his vehicle, but let's run the plates of each car here in case he borrowed a car or has obtained a rental."

"Where did the two old guys go?" Sienna glanced at Raelyn. "I hope they weren't driving."

"They walked that way," Raelyn gestured to the south. "I wouldn't have let them drive, but I'm sure they're looking for another bar."

With a nod, she listened as Zeke called in the plate numbers to the dispatcher. The process of verifying the car owners took several minutes. When Zeke finished, he looked dejected. "I should have gotten the IDs for the two old guys. Pretty sure two of the cars belong to them. A Larry Bellows and Edward Jenkins. The third car belongs to a guy by the name of Timothy Iverson. I don't know if Ken Holt borrowed Iverson's car or if the vehicle owner was smart enough to leave the car here to take a rideshare home."

"Call Flynn, see if he can dig into Iverson," Sienna suggested. "Maybe we can head over to Iverson's residence. Maybe Ken lives with him or rents a room from him or something like that."

Zeke took her advice on calling Flynn but didn't look interested in heading out to the address associated with the Iverson vehicle. "Hey, Flynn, check this guy out. See what you can come up with." There was a long pause, then Zeke spoke again. "Nope. Holt took off when we showed up. Bolted out the back of the bar as if the place was on fire. It's my fault. I should have had Raelyn stationed back there."

Sienna knew Zeke was blaming himself to take the pressure off her. But it didn't work. The truth was, if Zeke and Raelyn had been here alone, they would have been able to talk to Ken Holt before he knew what was happening.

The only good news was that Ken had likely run away because he was responsible for taking those shots at her. He was the gunman hired by Josh to stalk her.

Now they just had to find him. Again.

"Thanks, Flynn. Keep me updated." Zeke pocketed his phone and took her arm. "Let's get back to the SUV."

"You want me to stick around?" Raelyn asked. "Maybe your guy will return."

Zeke considered that for a moment. The way he glanced at her made Sienna realize how much he wished he could stay instead. "Maybe just for an hour or two. I know you have a family at home."

"No problem. I'll let Isaiah and Leon know." Raelyn smiled. "I doubt your guy Holt will come back; he must realize we're cops. But if he does, I'll grab him."

"Thanks, Rae." Zeke subtly drew her toward the SUV. Sienna didn't protest, she'd done enough damage for one evening.

A long silence stretched between them as Zeke started the car and pulled away from the curb. To her surprise, he drove slowly around the block, raking his gaze over the area as if searching for Ken.

"I'm sorry." She couldn't take the silence for another moment. "I know Ken's getting away is my fault. I honestly didn't expect him to bolt like that."

"It's not your fault, it's mine." Zeke's tone was clipped. "I should have anticipated his reaction. Don't worry, he escaped tonight, but we'll get him."

She bit her lower lip, wishing things were different.

Obviously, she wasn't a cop and needed to stop pretending she was. Finding and arresting Ken was Zeke's job, not hers.

Wallowing in guilt wasn't going to help. Ignoring the rumbling in her stomach, she searched their surroundings, too, hoping and praying that Ken was hiding nearby.

He wasn't.

"Do you have the address for Tim Iverson?" She glanced at Zeke's solemn profile. "It wouldn't hurt to swing by the place."

He scowled but nodded. "It's not that far away, and it's in a nicer neighborhood. But it's not like we have any evidence he's associated with Holt."

"I understand, but maybe we'll spot Ken hanging out there." She was doing her best to salvage the situation. "It can't hurt to look, right?"

He sighed. "Fine. We'll drive past on our way back to the safe house."

"Okay." Maybe it was a fool's errand, but she knew Zeke didn't want to return to the safe house without having anything to show for their excursion.

As Zeke navigated the streets, it was obvious they were going from a somewhat sketchy neighborhood to a nicely maintained one. The houses were larger and sported lawns that were well cared for.

"It's the third from the corner," Zeke said with a nod to the right. "The tan brick house with brown and white trim."

"I see it." The home was larger than she expected. She was so focused on the house that she was startled when Zeke's phone rang.

"Hey, Flynn, did you find something?" Zeke hit the brake and pulled over to the side of the street mere feet from the house owned by Timothy Iverson. "I'm at the guy's residence now. Doesn't seem to be the type that would rent rooms to guys like Holt."

She strained to listen to Flynn's side of the conversation. She only caught a couple of words, but it soon became clear that Iverson was the bar owner.

"Interesting that he owns the bar, but I wonder where he is?" Zeke stared up at the house. "I'd think he'd be at the bar if his car was there."

"Not if he drank too much to drive," she said in a whisper. "Maybe you should knock at the door to let him know his bartender took off."

Zeke's scowl deepened, but then he nodded. "Stay here. If the owner was drinking, he could be irritable."

"I will." As Zeke slid out of the driver's seat, she hoped Tim Iverson was a nice and amicable drunk.

She'd given up drinking even before she'd gotten pregnant. Josh turned mean when he drank, and initially his abuse had been verbal. That should have been her cue to leave, but she'd foolishly hoped that if he'd only stop drinking, he'd be better.

Instead, the situation had gotten worse.

Shaking off the memories, she watched as Zeke stood at the front door waiting for someone to respond to his knock. Eventually, the front door opened, revealing a small woman. She and Zeke spoke for a few minutes, then Zeke headed back to the car.

"He wasn't home?" she asked.

"Apparently, he was sleeping," Zeke said with a shrug. "Sleeping off his overindulgence, I'm sure. That was his wife, Nancy. She appreciated hearing about the bartender but came across as eager to get rid of me."

"She's probably embarrassed by her husband's drinking." At least, she had always felt like Josh's bad habits were somehow her fault. It took time for her to understand he was responsible for his own decisions.

Especially when he'd started hitting her.

"At least we know Holt isn't living there." Zeke pulled away from the curb and followed the signs to the interstate. "Time to get back to the safe house."

She sat back in her seat, knowing there was nothing more to be done here. Causing Ken to take off was not the outcome they'd been hoping for. Maybe the cops would find Ken sometime tonight. But if they didn't?

A sense of unease washed over her. The deadline she'd given Zeke was ticking by faster than she'd expected. Two days sounded like a lot. But it wasn't.

Especially since they were no closer to getting to the bottom of these attacks.

ZEKE TRIED to shake off the sense of failure as he drove to the safe house. He hated knowing he let Ken Holt slip through his fingers.

And he had no one to blame but himself.

Yet he needed to let it go. To regroup and go back to investigating the guy on social media. He'd found Holt at the Wooden Nickel, maybe he could find something else to link to the guy.

If the cops didn't pick him up first.

Digging out his phone, he called Flynn. "We're on our way back. Would you mind tossing the pizzas into the oven?"

"Will do," Flynn agreed. "Sorry things didn't work out."

"Yeah, thanks." He dropped the phone into the

cupholder. "I'll keep digging into Holt's background after we eat."

"I can help," Sienna offered.

He glanced at her. "I'm not angry or upset. Losing Holt was my fault, not yours. I'm confident we'll find him."

"It's nice of you to take the blame, but I know this would have gone down differently if I hadn't insisted on coming along," Sienna said.

"He did react rather unexpectedly to seeing you." Zeke replayed those moments in his head. Holt's gaze had widened with shocked recognition seconds before he disappeared through the door behind the bar. "He never anticipated we'd show up at his place of employment."

"I wonder if he'll call Josh to let him know," Sienna said, her tone thoughtful. "If so, that might be enough for Josh to call off additional attacks."

"That's possible." Now that they had the safe house, he doubted there would be any more attacks. Allenton would have to find them first. "Regardless of what Josh does from this point forward, we'll keep working the case. No matter what, I plan to hold your ex-husband accountable for his actions."

"All I want is for him to leave me and Bailey alone," she said with a sigh. "I don't understand why he can't just move forward with his life, leaving us out of it."

"I don't know." In his job, he saw all kinds of people. Some were good people who'd gotten themselves into a bad situation. Some were intent on doing evil no matter what.

He suspected Josh Allenton fell into the latter category.

They rode the rest of the way to the safe house in silence. He called Flynn to ask him to open the garage door. Once they were parked, he followed Sienna inside. The spicy scent of pepperoni and cheese made his stomach growl.

"The pizzas will be ready shortly," Flynn said. Glancing into the living room, he took note of Taylor playing with Bailey. Bailey lit up when she saw her mother and toddled toward Sienna. She lifted the little girl into her arms, hugging and kissing her before setting her back on her feet. Bailey didn't hesitate to go back to playing with the building blocks Taylor had spread out on the floor.

He cocked an eyebrow at Flynn who shrugged as if to say nothing untoward had happened with Taylor and Bailey while they were gone.

He knew Taylor hadn't called ahead to warn Ken Holt. For one thing, he hadn't given her a disposable phone yet. For another, it was obvious Holt had been caught completely off guard by their unexpected arrival.

Sienna stepped into the kitchen, drew on the oven mitts, and peeked inside the oven. "They look great," she said, closing the door. "Five minutes should do it."

"Thanks." He dropped into the chair beside Flynn. "I stopped by to see Iverson, but he was sleeping it off."

"Not surprised." Flynn gestured to the screen. "His bar isn't doing well, probably because he's spending all his time drinking his profits. Looks like there are several financial judgments against Iverson. He probably owes more than what the place is worth."

Money could be a powerful motivator to turn criminal, but Iverson had been home sleeping while Holt had been the one to take off upon seeing Sienna. He didn't see how Iverson could be involved. "Thanks for checking him out. Looks like we should stay focused on finding Ken Holt."

"I agree. I've been digging through his social media— nice catch on the T-shirt logo by the way—but so far haven't found anything else." Flynn rubbed the back of his neck. "We can start over after we eat."

"It's my problem, I can take over from here," Zeke said. "You look like you could use some rest."

"Hey, this is a cakewalk compared to my usual shift," Flynn joked. "It was nice of Rhy to assign me here to guard duty."

Zeke knew he owed Rhy and Joe big time for their support.

"Dinner's ready," Sienna announced a few minutes later. "Taylor, did you and Bailey eat already?"

"We did," Taylor called back. "Flynn wanted to wait for you, so there's half a cold pizza in the fridge."

"Okay, then I'll portion these out for us, then." As she spoke, Sienna used the pizza cutter to slice the pies into triangles. Then she placed several slices on plates and carried them to the table.

"I'd like to say grace." Sienna glanced between him and Flynn once they were seated around the table. When he nodded and bowed his head, Flynn mirroring his actions, she said, "Dear Lord Jesus. We thank You for this food we are blessed to eat. We ask You to continue keeping us all safe in Your care. Amen."

"Amen," he and Flynn echoed. Then Flynn added Roscoe's line. "Dig in."

"It's not the same without a Texas drawl," Zeke protested.

"Hey, speaking of Roscoe, I forgot to tell you, he texted me earlier. Libby is in labor." Flynn grinned. "Hard to believe Roscoe is going to be a father."

"Wow, I'm really happy for him." Zeke knew Roscoe was head over heels in love with Libby. "I can't lie, I'm really glad he agreed to stick around here rather than moving back to Texas."

"Same," Flynn agreed.

"Roscoe and Libby?" Sienna looked confused. "Are they both part of your team?"

"Just Roscoe," he said. "There are nine members total, and of those, we have three female officers: Raelyn, Jina, and Cassidy. Libby's a schoolteacher and recently married Roscoe."

"I see." She nodded. "It's nice that you are all so friendly."

He was blessed to be a part of this closely knit team. "Yeah. It's nice to know that we can count on each other no matter what is going down."

"That reminds me, did Raelyn stay at the bar to keep an eye on things?" Flynn asked.

"She did. But I'm sure Holt is smart enough not to go back." He grimaced and reached for his phone. "I'll call and tell her to head home."

"Let her know about Libby," Flynn said.

He nodded. When Raelyn answered, he said, "I take it there's been no sign of Holt?"

"Nothing. A few of the regulars stopped by, though. They seemed confused to find the place shut down." There was a hint of humor in her tone. "The two old guys haven't come back, though."

"Flynn heard that Libby's in labor," he said. "Which means Roscoe's paternity leave starts tomorrow. I'm calling to tell you to head home. I stopped by to chat with the bar owner, but he was already sleeping. I doubt Holt is worried about losing his job. Sounds like his boss spends most of his days drinking anyway."

"I was planning to head home. Isaiah just let me know that he has dinner ready," she admitted. "I feel bad how this went down. If you need more support, let me know. I'm here to help if needed."

"Thanks, Rae. Enjoy your evening." He ended the call with a sense of defeat. He'd royally botched their best lead.

It burned to know Holt was in the wind.

He took another bite of his pepperoni pizza, trying to come up with another lead. From the very beginning, they'd been reacting to threats—the threatening notes, the brick through the window of the rental house in White Gull Bay, and the gunfire on the road and within the Sinatra Music Center.

They needed to do a better job of investigating this thing. Where would Holt go if he needed to disappear? Would he really call Josh and tell him that Sienna showed up at the bar? Or would he see that as a failure that he'd rather keep hidden from his boss?

Probably the latter. Especially if Josh promised some money up front with more to follow once the job was complete.

And what was the job exactly? The attacks had gone well beyond an attempt to get the threats on record.

Did Josh want to scare Sienna into canceling her show? Or did he plan to set Ken Holt up to kill her?

Killing Sienna would not necessarily lead to his obtaining custody of Bailey. And why did he want joint custody so badly?

He couldn't help feeling as if they were missing something.

"You mentioned you're not getting any child support from Allenton, right?" he asked.

"I agreed to forfeit that in exchange for full custody, yes," Sienna said. "Josh has no financial reason to seek joint custody."

"Yeah, I keep coming back to that," he admitted. "I can understand his wanting some sort of revenge, but normally in those cases, the satisfaction comes from doing the deed directly. Not usually by paying someone else to do the dirty work."

"Maybe not, but once Josh's parents became rich, he began paying people to do everything for him." She shook her head. "He enjoyed directing others to do his bidding."

Was that really what was driving Josh? "What happens if he gets joint custody, though? Does he get child support from you?"

"No, why would he?" Sienna looked confused. "He has more money than I do."

"His parents have more money than you do," he corrected, warming to the theory. "Josh doesn't make any of his own money, does he?"

She frowned. "I don't know if he's still in the music industry. I haven't paid any attention to his career since I'm on a completely different path now."

"Okay, hear me out. If Josh can get joint custody of Bailey, maybe he'll ask for child support payments as well."

"I guess he could," Sienna admitted. "But I'm not sure why he'd bother. His parents give him whatever he wants. A car, a house, you name it, they've given it to him."

He frowned, realizing she was right. Based on what she was describing, it made more sense for her ex-husband to move on with his life. "I don't know," he finally said. "I just can't see the end game here."

Bailey began to fuss, causing Sienna to jump up from her seat, leaving her half-eaten pizza behind. "I'll take her."

"No, finish eating," Taylor insisted. "Let me give her a bath. You can put her to bed."

"I—okay." Sienna sank back into her chair. "Thanks."

"Of course." Taylor carried Bailey to the bathroom, promising her fun in the tub.

"I guess I'm not used to having a nanny," Sienna admitted. "I know I need someone to watch Bailey while I'm performing, and it seemed like a good idea to have someone here full time." Her gaze followed Taylor and Bailey down the hall. "Now I'm second-guessing myself."

"I'm sure it's not easy being a single parent," he said. He finished his pizza and stood to get seconds. It was plain as far as toppings went, but it hit the spot.

"Well, she won't be a single parent for long once you two get married," Flynn pointed out as he rose for seconds too. "I'm sure you can work out your schedules so that you won't need a full-time nanny for much longer."

Sienna hesitated, then nodded. "Yes, of course, you're right." She smiled brightly as she took his hand. "Zeke will be an amazing dad."

He had no idea what to say to that. Thankfully, his disposable phone rang. Praying the cops had picked up Ken Holt, he quickly answered. "Hawthorne."

"Zeke? It's Steele. I'm afraid I have bad news."

It took him a moment to understand why he was hearing from Steele. Until he remembered Steele lived in White Gull Bay. His stomach sank. "What is it?"

"I happened to be driving past the rental house your fiancée was using. It's surrounded by police cars, so I stopped in, explaining I lived in the area and was concerned about what was going on." There was a pause, before Steele continued. "The local police got an anonymous tip regarding a burglar. They found a dead body in the house. He's your BOLO, Ken Holt."

"No way." Zeke had not expected that. He glanced at Sienna, then at Flynn. "How did Holt die?"

"Gunshot wound to the chest," Steele said. "From what I saw, the shooter was up close and personal when he killed him."

He sighed, knowing that not only would this end up in the newspapers, but their only lead on the shooter was dead.

Taken out by yet another shooter.

What on earth was going on?

CHAPTER NINE

Sienna gripped the edge of the table for support as she struggled to make sense of what Zeke had said. Ken Holt was dead? How was that possible? It had been less than two hours since she saw him standing behind the bar at the Wooden Nickel.

The brief glimpse of him flashed in her mind. She had assumed Ken had taken off because he was afraid of being arrested, but now she wasn't so sure. Maybe Ken was worried about something else.

Like failing in his mission to cause her grief.

Had Josh killed him? Was her ex-husband so determined to seek revenge on her that he'd killed a man? Not just any man, but his former friend? She could almost imagine how it may have played out. Ken had run away from the bar, then called Josh demanding to know what to do. Josh had agreed to meet with him, then had killed him.

Ken Holt's murder changed everything. This was no longer a simple custody case. Josh had crossed a line.

And she feared Josh believed there was no going back.

"Sienna? Are you okay?"

She realized Zeke had called her name several times. Even Flynn was looking at her in concern. "No, how can anyone be okay after this?"

Zeke and Flynn exchanged a quick glance. Then Flynn stood and gathered their empty plates together. "I'll start the dishes."

"We'll make sure you're not connected to this incident in any way." Zeke covered her hand in his. "You left the rental property late on Monday night."

She shook her head. "The police have to be involved now. A man has been brutally murdered. There's no brushing something of this magnitude under the rug." She shivered. "I just can't believe Ken is dead."

"I know." Zeke's expression was grim. "Steele thinks Ken knew his killer; he was shot in the chest at close range."

"You think Josh killed him." She pushed the sentence through a tight throat.

"Maybe." Zeke shrugged. "We should be able to figure out if your ex-husband left California to come here. That will help."

Josh's parents were wealthy, but not to the point of having their own private plane. Still, she wasn't convinced Josh would have left LA to come here without having some way of covering his tracks. After a long moment, a horrible thought struck. "Could chartering a private plane to Milwaukee help Josh stay off the radar?"

"It's possible," Zeke admitted. "But even private planes have to land at one of the hangars at the Milwaukee airport. There are other smaller airports, but he'd need a decent-sized plane to get him here from across the country. I'll have Gabe get information on all private flights in and out of the city. Maybe I'll include Madison, too, just to cover all bases."

It sounded like a monumental task, one that wouldn't be accomplished in a week, much less one day. Once again, she was torn by indecision. Was there any reason to stick around? Was it better for everyone if she disappeared with Bailey now rather than waiting?

Lord Jesus, guide me! Show me the way!

"Mama?" Bailey walked toward her wearing pink footie pajamas. Tugging her hand from Zeke's, she scooped the little girl into her arms and held her close.

Drawing in the sweet scent of baby shampoo helped steady her nerves. It was too late tonight to make any decisions about staying or going, but tomorrow?

First thing in the morning, she'd need to begin planning her exit strategy. She didn't want to break her contract and refund the money for the tickets, but nothing was more important than her daughter.

"Time for bed, young lady," she said with mock sternness. Rising to her feet, she carried the little girl to the bedroom she'd used earlier for Bailey's naptime. She would sleep next to her daughter, leaving Taylor, Zeke, and Flynn to decide who should get the other two bedrooms.

"Sing! Sing!" Bailey said as she settled on the edge of the bed.

"You need to lie down first," she said, arranging the pillows to keep her daughter from falling off. She had gotten into the habit of singing Bailey to sleep, which probably wasn't as good for her as reading a bedtime story.

But singing Christian hymns as a bedtime ritual helped Sienna feel closer to God in a way that prayer didn't always accomplish. She had come to accept that God wanted her to use her voice to proclaim His name. And praising Him while feeling close to the Lord was more important than preparing Bailey for school.

Especially now.

Bailey snuggled with her stuffed elephant as she began to sing her daughter's favorite, *Jesus Loves Me*. Sometimes the little girl tried to sing along, but other times, like tonight, it didn't take long for the little girl's eyelids to slowly droop and close as if she was losing herself in the song.

The way Sienna was.

After finishing the final notes, tears pricked at her eyes. She watched Bailey sleeping before slowly standing to leave the room. She stopped abruptly when she saw Zeke leaning against the doorframe, obviously having been there the entire time.

"Beautiful," he whispered as she approached. From the admiration shining in his eyes, she wasn't sure he meant her or the song.

"Thank you." She drew him away from the door so she could close it.

"Do you sing to her every night?" Zeke asked.

"Most nights. If I'm home." She tried to smile but couldn't. "In truth, doing so calms me as much as it does her."

There was a long moment as Zeke searched her gaze before he spoke. "Please don't leave yet. You promised to give me two days."

He could read her thoughts better than anyone else. Even her brother, Luke. She wished Luke was there now to help her decide what to do.

"I haven't made any plans," she finally said as they returned to the living room. "But if Josh has really killed a man . . ." She didn't finish her thought.

It was terrifying to think she and Bailey could be next. Something along the lines of if he couldn't have their daughter, then no one could.

"If we can prove that, Josh will be in jail for the rest of his life," Zeke said. "Don't you see? Your ex is growing desperate. I think he killed Ken Holt to prevent him from telling us that Josh hired him to stalk you."

She wanted to believe the police would uncover the proof they needed to charge Josh with murder, but she didn't. The Josh she knew would find a way to cover his tracks. Money had a way of making witnesses suffer amnesia.

Even his parents would support him in every way possible. She firmly believed they'd lie to the police and in court if necessary to cover for him.

After all, they'd denied knowing anything about Josh's abuse, even though she had confronted them with the truth.

"Trust me, Sienna. I won't let you down," Zeke murmured.

"I do trust you, but that's not the issue." She sank into the sofa feeling exhausted. "Bailey is the most important person in my life. I can't allow Josh to hurt her."

"He won't." Zeke spoke with a confidence she wished she could share. "Killing Ken Holt was his first mistake. He overplayed his hand tonight. No way will a slew of cops ignore a cold-blooded murder."

"What if he finds some way to implicate me?" She lifted her gaze to his. "Dirk booked the rental house under my name."

"You've been with me and Raelyn during the time frame of the murder, so that won't happen," he assured her. "Besides, Steele is working with the local district cops to keep you out of it. He contacted Rhy who is chatting with their captain as we speak." He hesitated, then added, "They'll need to interview you, though."

And that was the problem. "Which is exactly what Josh

wants. My name in a police report. I'm sure he'll see my name associated with a murder investigation as being a better reason to give up custody of my daughter compared to being the victim of stalker-like notes and petty vandalism."

"His name will be featured in a police report soon enough," Zeke said. "Give us time to follow up on a few things."

Time. She sighed and nodded. Zeke was a difficult man to resist.

In more ways than one.

"Thank you." He smiled. "I know we'll get to the bottom of this."

She desperately wanted to believe him. "I hope so." Sitting next to him like this made her yearn to have it all. Her career, her daughter, and maybe even a man like Zeke.

But she was afraid the mistake she made in marrying Josh Allenton was too much to overcome.

FROM THE MOMENT Sienna had listened to his call with Steele, Zeke had known she was planning to run. To find a way to get a couple of fake passports and leave the country to disappear forever.

The worst part? He was tempted to help her do that.

Despite being duty bound to uphold the law, he could easily understand Sienna's dilemma. It wasn't easy to stand and fight against those with money and power.

He slid his arm around her shoulder and drew her close, wishing there was more he could do or say to reassure her they were on the right path. Listening to her sing to Bailey only reinforced how important it was for her to be allowed to raise her daughter without interference from her ex. For her to share her talent with others.

God was watching over them. Zeke prayed God would also give him the wisdom and guidance he needed to arrest Allenton.

"Oh, Zeke." Sienna's whisper sent waves of awareness zipping down his spine. She turned her face into the hollow of his shoulder, her hand coming up to rest in the center of his chest. He wondered if she could feel the thundering beat of his heart. "I wish . . ."

He pressed a kiss to her temple. "It's going to be okay. Trust in me, my team, and the process."

"I'll try." She rested against him for a long moment. Then she lifted her head and kissed him. The rational part of his brain told him she meant it to be a kiss between friends, but the moment their lips touched, the embrace changed.

He tried to pull back, but Sienna nestled closer, deepening their kiss. Their embrace fried his brain cells. Only an earthquake could have ended this kiss.

Wisconsin didn't have earthquakes.

"Zeke?" Flynn's voice was almost as annoying as an earthquake. "Zeke? Rhy's on the line."

Rhy. His boss. With regret he pulled away. "Coming," he managed in a guttural tone.

"Better hurry," Flynn said.

"Good night, Zeke." Sienna appeared flustered by their embrace as she sat up and smoothed a hand over her hair. "We'll talk tomorrow."

"Good night, Sienna." It was all he could do not to kiss her again. Tearing himself away from her, he headed into the kitchen.

Ignoring the arched expression in Flynn's eyes, he

picked up the disposable phone. Praying his voice sounded more normal, he said, "Hey, Rhy. What's up?"

"I've convinced the White Gull Bay police to keep the murder investigation under wraps," Rhy said. "At least for now. They're more than a little interested in speaking to Sienna's ex-husband, though. And they'd like to interview her too."

"I know." Zeke didn't see a way around that. "Maybe we can arrange to meet with them at our precinct? Just to give her some distance from White Gull Bay?"

"I'll see if they'll go along with that," Rhy said. "Flynn mentioned you, Sienna, and Raelyn went out to speak with the victim?"

"Yeah." He quickly ran through a high-level description of the event. "I take full responsibility for letting him escape. If I had anticipated him bolting, he'd still be alive."

"Don't beat yourself up," Rhy advised. "Raelyn could have gone around back without you saying anything."

"My plan, my failure," he said.

"Get over it, you didn't kill the guy. Unfortunately, there was no phone found at the scene of the crime. The detectives assigned to the case will get Holt's cell phone records, but if he was using a disposable phone, there likely won't be anything to lead back to Allenton."

"Yeah, I know." He raked a hand through his hair. "We don't know where he's been staying either. Other than somewhere off-grid," he said.

"The detectives on scene found Ken Holt's car in the garage of the rental property," Rhy said. "They think he may have stayed there at least for one night."

"That's interesting." He could imagine Holt tossing the brick through the window, then watching as he packed up Sienna, Taylor, and Bailey to get them out of there. But to actually move into the place in their absence? That took some nerve. "I'm surprised he'd do that if the goal was to get the police to respond to the vandalism."

"The locals did respond, didn't see anyone, and dismissed it as a teenage prank," Rhy said. "Their theory is that Ken Holt moved into the place right after that. The broken window was removed and replaced with particle board."

Zeke sighed. "Do they have anything else?"

"Not at this time, but the city of White Gull Bay doesn't have much in the way of homicides, so the detectives are all over this." Rhy sounded tired. "Like I said, they're willing to play along for now."

"Great. Do they have my number to set up the interview?" Zeke asked.

"No, I asked them to work with me. I'll contact Detective Plato in the morning with a time for the interview. Say nine o'clock?"

"Nine works, thanks, Rhy." He ended the call and set the phone back on the table. "We need to keep digging. There has to be a way to tie this murder to Allenton."

"No one is going to stop working the case," Flynn assured him. "But you need to be careful. I've watched our teammates get emotionally involved to the point they almost got themselves killed."

Zeke had seen that too. Yet now that he was the one involved, it was easier to understand. "I love her, Flynn."

"Your engagement is real?" Flynn looked surprised.

"Not exactly, but it has to appear that way to the world." He dropped into the kitchen chair beside his friend. "I love her, but she sees me as a friend."

"Funny, that kiss looked more than friendly," Flynn teased.

It had felt like more than just friends to him, too, but it was time to change the subject. "I'm going to keep poring through social media posts. If you want to take the third bedroom, that's fine with me. I'll use the sofa."

"Suit yourself." Flynn yawned. "We should be safe here."

"Yeah." Zeke couldn't ignore his shrinking time frame. "Get some sleep. I'll need you to stay here with Taylor and Bailey so we can be interviewed by the White Gull Bay detectives."

"I figured." Flynn rose. "But you need to get some sleep too."

"I will." Zeke knew he was right. He'd already made one major mistake in letting Holt escape. He couldn't afford to make another.

He worked until the words blurred on the screen, then stretched out on the sofa. It seemed like only an hour later when he awoke.

A glance at his watch indicated it was six in the morning. Somehow, he'd slept all night. Too bad he didn't feel rested.

Coffee would help.

After brewing a pot, he sat down with a full mug and picked up where he'd left off. He'd tried everything he could think of to identify additional connections to Ken Holt but hadn't found anything useful.

No address, no additional places of employment. As a last resort, he decided to see if he could find any girlfriends that they could talk to.

But if the guy was in a romantic relationship, there was no sign of it on his social media pages.

He worked for about twenty minutes before everyone

began to stir. First Flynn, then Taylor, and finally Sienna and Bailey were up.

"I'll make breakfast," Taylor offered. "I hope everyone likes eggs because that's about all that's in the fridge."

"Works for me," Zeke said.

"We'll order groceries for the rest of the day," Flynn added. "I was going to suggest that last night but got distracted."

Yeah, dead bodies had a way of sidetracking things. He moved the computer to make more room at the kitchen table. Then he filled several mugs of coffee and set about making another pot.

He had a feeling this would be a long day and that he'd need all the coffee he could get.

"We need to be at the precinct by nine," he told Sienna. "Flynn will stay here with Taylor and Bailey."

"Sure, I understand." She didn't look as if she'd gotten much sleep either. The stress of the interview with the police and the shrinking time frame left to work on the case was wearing on her too.

He'd hoped they'd be further along by now. Instead, things had taken a turn for the worse with Holt's murder.

After eating eggs for breakfast, he took a quick shower, more to get rid of the cobwebs than anything. Feeling better, he joined the others in the kitchen. Sienna had showered as well, her thick hair framing her face.

He eyed the coffee, considering one for the road. A quick peek through the cupboards squashed that notion. Not a to-go cup to be had.

"We'll be back soon," he told Flynn, holding the garage door for Sienna. "I'll keep you updated."

"No problem." Flynn was seated at the table working on

the computer. He agreed to focus on Brett Voss since Holt was proving to be a dead end.

Sienna didn't say anything until they were out on the road. "I need to contact Dirk using my regular phone once we're at the precinct. My morning show interview is tomorrow. I'm sure he wants to update me about that."

Taking it as a good sign she was talking about the morning show interview, he nodded. "Sure, that's a good plan. What about your rehearsal later tonight?" She had one slotted in on her original schedule. "Are you still planning to do that?"

"No need." She shrugged. "I know the songs well enough."

And just like that, his hopes plummeted. She had no intention of going on with the tour. They were silent during the rest of the trip to the precinct. As before, he parked in the back and took Sienna in through the rear entrance that typically only officers used. She stood outside for a moment to power up her phone. She called her manager, but Dirk must not have answered, so she left a message.

They were ten minutes early, but as he led Sienna through the maze of cubicles, he could see Rhy speaking with two cops dressed in suits.

Sienna saw the White Gull Bay detectives, too, her blue gaze apprehensive. "Just be honest and upfront with them," he advised.

She nodded. He opened the door and waved to her to enter first.

"Sienna Reynolds, this is Detective Plato and Detective Marks," Rhy said by way of introduction. "Detectives, this is Sienna Reynolds and one of my officers, Zeke Hawthorne. He and Sienna are recently engaged."

"Oh yeah?" Detective Plato eyed him curiously. Zeke

did his best to appear nonchalant about the whole thing. The questions started out easily enough, placing Sienna's name, address, and contact information on record. But when they asked about why she left the rental house despite having booked it for the week, a hint of panic flashed in her eyes.

He wanted to intervene, but she pulled herself together to explain about the brick coming through the window. "I was convinced some neighborhood kid had tossed it, but Zeke felt we should move to a different location." She smiled, and added, "I value his advice related to safety. You can't be too careful these days."

The questions became more pointed when they brought up her relationship with the deceased.

"I have not spoken to Ken Holt in years," Sienna answered honestly. "He was my ex-husband's friend, not mine. I never cared much for him, but I certainly didn't have a reason to hurt him."

"We've been in touch with your ex-husband; he's in LA," Detective Marks said. "He told us he hasn't seen or spoken to Ken Holt since he relocated there."

While that was what he'd expected, he had to hide a stab of disappointment. "How do you know for sure Allenton is in LA?"

Detective Plato shrugged. "We don't, but he gave us the name of his buddy Shawn Court who will supposedly vouch for him."

Vouch? Or lie? Zeke glanced at Rhy, but his boss's expression didn't reveal his thoughts.

The questions went on for almost a full hour. The detectives pressed him on the BOLO and didn't look happy to know that he'd found Holt at the Wooden Nickel, only to allow him to escape out the back.

"You can try the bar owner, a guy named Timothy Iverson," he said. "I spoke to his wife, Nancy, last night, but she didn't seem to know anything. The bar isn't doing well financially, and I suspect the guy sits and drinks all day, but he should be sober by now."

"He's on our list after this," Plato said. "You're sure you didn't see which way our vic went after leaving the bar?"

"If I had, I would have followed him," Zeke said. "I wanted to talk to him about his relationship with Sienna's ex-husband."

"All of this is over a custody dispute?" Marks asked. "Seems over the top."

"Josh is a very controlling man," Sienna said in a subdued tone. "His goal isn't custody, but to watch me suffer."

Her quiet dignity rendered both detectives quiet for a long moment. Moments later, they ended the interview.

"We may have follow-up questions," Plato said.

"You can reach them through me." Rhy's tone was firm. "Thanks for coming out."

The detectives glanced at each other, then left. Zeke waited until they were gone to ask, "Did Gabe come up with anything on Allenton? Or Brett Voss?"

"Not much," Rhy said. "You know about the charges he found on Holt. Voss also has an old drug charge on his record from when Brett and Allenton were in college, but he got off with a slap on the wrist and community service."

"Drugs while they were in college?" Sienna frowned. "I didn't know anything about that."

Zeke felt certain there was a lot she didn't know about her ex but didn't mention it. He filled Rhy on the lack of information he'd gotten via social media, then led the way to the rear exit door.

They were heading to the car when Sienna stopped and looked down at her phone. "Oh, wait. This is Dirk." Per their previous agreement, she only used it when they were at the precinct or the music center. Not at the safe house. She frowned, then lowered the device. "That's weird. He didn't leave a message."

He was about to suggest she try calling him back when the sharp crack of gunfire rang out. Heart in his throat, he yanked her down and covered her body with his.

CHAPTER TEN

One second she was looking down at her phone, the next she was down on the ground beneath Zeke's muscled frame. While she couldn't see anything, shouts echoed from the police precinct as footsteps pounded the pavement.

"To the right," Zeke shouted. "The black car!"

She squirmed, trying to get out from beneath him. After a long moment, Zeke stood, giving her room to breathe. He grasped her arm to help her upright.

"Are you okay?" He ran his hands up and down her arms as if to reassure himself there were no bullet wounds. "You weren't hit?"

"I'm fine. What about you?" She was humbled by the way he'd put himself in the line of fire. She didn't see any sign of blood. Not like when Flynn had gotten nicked at the City Central Hotel.

"Not hit." His tone was curt. "Just angry that this guy had the nerve to take a shot at us here outside the precinct."

"How did he know we were here?" Her gaze landed on her cracked phone lying on the ground. "My phone? He tracked my phone?"

"It wasn't the first time." Zeke bent and scooped it up. He stared down at the screen for a moment, then at her. "Your manager, Dirk. He didn't answer either of your calls. Then suddenly someone is shooting at us."

Hard to argue Zeke's logic. Normally, Dirk would be quick to respond to her calls. Then again, she hadn't powered up her phone in hours. Maybe Dirk was angry with her for shutting him out.

"I don't know what to think." Taking the phone, she quickly powered it down, then handed it back to him. "Ditch it if you want, I don't care."

He nodded, then slid his arm around her shoulders to give her a quick hug. "I'm sorry. I know it's hard to accept a friend's betrayal."

Dirk wasn't a friend, but he was important to her. Obviously, moving forward with the tour wasn't going to work. Even if Zeke could prove Dirk was involved and have him arrested, who would be able to pick up where Dirk left off? There wasn't time to find another manager.

She didn't like it, but she had to accept that her future as a Christian singer would be short-lived.

As in nonexistent.

"You both okay?" Rhy jogged over to them.

"Yeah. What about the black car?" Zeke gestured to the right. "Anyone catch up to it?"

"Not yet." Rhy sighed and rubbed the back of his neck. "I don't like this."

"It's my fault," Sienna said. "I used my phone to contact my manager. I guess he's been tracking my phone for my ex-husband."

Rhy glanced at Zeke who nodded. "That's the working theory. I think we should go back inside and give Dirk Green a call." Zeke frowned. "Is he even in Wisconsin? I'd like to set up a face-to-face meeting with him, preferably here at the precinct."

"Yes, he's in town, staying in a hotel near the music center." Maybe Zeke was right about setting up a meeting with Dirk. After everything that had happened, including Ken Holt's murder, this nightmare had to end.

Soon. Before anyone else got hurt.

"Let's get you inside." Zeke tugged on her arm. She didn't resist, knowing he was only looking out for her safety.

At the expense of his own.

Maybe it was time to change tactics. She could call her lawyer and accuse Josh of trying to kill her. He would deny it, but she could point out that he has the financial means and motive to pay someone to come after her.

Would the judge put the custody hearing on hold pending the outcome of the investigation? Possibly, since Josh had a history of physical abuse. If so, that could buy her some time.

Time to arrange a way for her and Bailey to disappear.

"Which hotel is Dirk staying at?" Zeke asked, settling in behind a computer.

"The Pfister," she admitted.

Zeke arched a brow. "Fancy."

She winced. "I'm paying for his stay." She'd personally thought it was a waste of money, but the old historic hotel was also a status symbol, one he couldn't resist. "He insisted he wanted to stay there because it was close to the venue."

"You didn't stay there," Zeke pointed out, bringing the hotel website up.

"We would have needed a large two-bedroom suite, and the rental house seemed easier." And cheaper, but that hadn't been the true deciding factor. It had been her hope to avoid getting more threatening letters.

So much for that plan.

"This is MPD Officer Hawthorne, I need to speak with one of your guests, a Mr. Dirk Green." Zeke's tone was polite but firm. "Yes, I'll hold."

She leaned forward, wishing he'd put the call on speaker. But it didn't matter.

"No answer in his room?" Zeke was saying. "I'd like to leave a message. Please ask him to call the MPD Seventh District at this number to speak with Officer Zeke Hawthorne. Thank you." After hanging up the phone, Zeke turned to her. "Any idea where he might be?"

"Possibly at the TV station to finalize details for the morning show interview." A shiver of apprehension washed over her. "Could he be in danger too?"

Zeke didn't answer for a long moment. "I don't know. I'm a little concerned at how quickly after our arrival at the Wooden Nickel that Ken Holt was murdered. Your ex has already silenced one witness. From that, I'd say anything is possible."

"We need to head over to the hotel." She tried to think back to the details Dirk had arranged. Had he mentioned his hotel room? She reached for her phone. "I might have his room number in an email from him."

"Hold on, why don't you access your email from this computer instead?" Zeke dropped her phone in the trash and stood to offer up his chair. "If you have his room number, we'll check it out."

"Okay." She honestly couldn't remember if he'd given it to her or not. At the time, she hadn't paid any attention since his room didn't impact her in any way. It took a moment for her to remember her password, then she logged in.

There were at least a dozen unread messages in her

inbox. Swallowing a flash of guilt, she realized she should have checked in before now.

Scanning the emails, she noticed several were from Dirk, one from her lawyer in the custody case, and yet others from the PR firm Dirk was using. She clicked on the email from her attorney first. Thankfully, there wasn't anything new to be concerned with; Marsha was simply reminding her of the court date.

As if I could forget, she thought as she clicked out.

"Dirk's room number?" Zeke said.

"Yeah, sorry." She opened Dirk's most recent email next. He was upset she hadn't answered any of his calls. She scrolled down to see his previous emails.

Then near the bottom, she found the one she was looking for. Dirk's room number. She sat back so Zeke could see the screen. "He's in suite 305."

"Great, I'm heading over." He jumped to his feet. "I'd like you to wait for us here."

She didn't want to wait, but remembering how she'd blown the visit to the Wooden Nickel gave her pause. "Zeke, I don't want to put you or anyone in danger, but Dirk is more likely to answer the door for me."

"I'm a cop. He'll answer the door," Zeke said.

"And if he doesn't?" She reached for the computer keyboard and double-checked the hotel registration. "He used my *Sienna!* business account to book the room. I think that allows me access to a room key."

Zeke scowled, then reluctantly nodded. "Okay, that works." He hesitated, then added, "Stay behind me as much as possible, okay? It shouldn't be dangerous to go to a hotel, but I want you to be prepared for anything."

"I understand." She wouldn't make the same mistake she had at the Wooden Nickel. "I won't get in your way."

He looked a bit skeptical but led the way back outside. Two officers came in as they were heading out.

"Did you lose the black car?" Zeke asked.

"Yeah, sorry. There was no rear plate either." One cop shook his head in disgust. "We've issued a BOLO for it. Hopefully, someone notices and pulls him over."

"Thanks." Zeke gave them a nod and then turned to her. "Please wait here while I get the SUV."

"Sure." She moved aside to allow the officers to head inside and scanned the parking lot as Zeke jogged to Flynn's SUV. She didn't see anything suspicious, but she hadn't noticed the gunman either.

The more she thought about Dirk working with Josh to locate her, the more her anger simmered. Dirk should know better than to believe anything Josh told him. Yet she also knew Dirk was easily swayed by money.

The more the better.

Zeke pulled up a few minutes later. He was quiet during the drive to the hotel. The historic hotel was impressive, and it made her wonder just how much staying here cost.

"Let's go to his room first," Zeke said, moving past the main desk as if they knew exactly where they were going.

"Okay." She turned toward the elevator and jabbed the button. "I'm going to assume it's on the third floor."

"You've never stayed here?" Zeke asked.

"Nope." She had preferred the modest but nice rental house. Up until the moment a brick came through the window.

Finding Dirk's room wasn't difficult. She quickened her pace when she saw a cleaning cart parked beside it. The door was ajar, so she pushed it open and breezed inside.

"Oh, hi," she greeted the maid with a cheerful smile.

"Don't mind me, I forgot something." She stood and scanned the room, grateful there was no sign of trouble. Dirk's suitcase was open, but empty. The maid eyed her suspiciously as she ducked into the bathroom in pretense of leaving something behind.

"Oh, here it is," she spoke loud enough for the maid to hear. Then emerged from the bathroom. "Thanks, sorry about that. Dirk's waiting for me at the TV studio."

A moment later, she was back in the hall where Zeke had waited. "I'm impressed you were able to pull that off," he said in a low voice. "See anything unusual inside?"

"No, it's a typical motel room. Well, nicer than most," she amended. "Remind me to never pursue an acting career. I'm not good at pretending." She glanced down at the beautiful engagement ring on her finger for a second, then did her best to ignore it. "Obviously, Dirk isn't here. Maybe he really is at the TV studio."

"Let's head back down to the lobby, maybe we'll catch him returning to his room." Zeke rested his hand in the small of her back as they returned to the elevator. "Whatever he's up to shouldn't take too long."

"Hopefully not meeting with Josh," she said as they stepped into the elevator. "I don't care what his good friend Shawn says, I'm convinced Josh is here in Milwaukee." As they emerged from the elevator and stepped into the grand lobby with the high ceilings and beautiful curved staircase leading to the grand ballroom, she had to admit that if Josh was in town, this was exactly the sort of place he'd stay.

Maybe hanging out in the lobby would be the best option. She followed Zeke to a set of plush chairs, silently praying that if Josh was in town, they'd find him here.

Putting an end to this once and for all.

ZEKE HAD to work hard to remain calm and relaxed as the minutes ticked by. He'd been encouraged to learn Dirk's room was empty and being serviced by the hotel staff. He hadn't anticipated Sienna would breeze in like she owned the place, but her pretense had worked to their advantage.

He'd half expected to find her manager dead in his room with a gunshot wound to the chest.

Like Ken Holt.

Thrusting that image aside, he scanned the faces of those coming and going in the plush hotel. Patience was not his strong suit, and when he caught a glimpse of a couple of star baseball players, he resisted the urge to ask for an autograph.

"We've been here an hour," Sienna said in a low voice. "How long do you plan to stick around?"

"As long as it takes." He had considered heading to the TV station, but Sienna's comment about Dirk meeting with Josh had convinced him that sticking around here was the better option.

Yet the seemingly endless waiting was wearing on him too.

He was about to suggest they head back to the precinct when a man walked in through the main doors. "Sienna? Is that you?"

"Hi, Dirk." She stood and would have headed over toward the guy if he hadn't grabbed her hand. She paused, waiting for Dirk to approach. "I'd like you to meet my fiancé, Zeke Hawthorne."

Dirk's eyes narrowed taking in Zeke's appearance, then he frowned. "Wait, aren't you the cop that left me a message?"

"Oh, so you did get that." Zeke stepped forward, putting himself between Dirk and Sienna, to shake the man's hand. He didn't see obvious signs of a weapon, and the cut of Dirk's suit was such that he would have noticed a shoulder harness. "Nice to meet you. We need a few minutes of your time."

"Where have you been, Sienna?" Dirk asked, ignoring Zeke. "I've called and emailed, without the courtesy of a response. I just met with the PR team at the TV station. They were wondering where you were."

"What time did you get to the TV station?" Zeke asked.

"Eight thirty, why?" Dirk scowled. "I don't understand how you and Sienna can be engaged. She wasn't dating anyone that I knew about."

"I prefer to keep my personal life private," Sienna said. "Zeke is an old family friend. And as he said, we need to talk."

"We can use my suite," Dirk said, seemingly less angry now that Sienna was there.

Zeke was tempted to push the issue of going to the precinct for the interview but decided against it. Dirk may not have answered his phone because he was at the TV station. And that also meant he wasn't the shooter.

Maybe talking to him here in a laid-back environment would be better. He glanced at Sienna, who frowned.

"Let's talk here in the lobby," she suggested.

Dirk glanced around, then walked toward a trio of chairs. "There's a lot we need to discuss," Dirk said, ignoring Zeke. "I have several more interviews set up, in Chicago and in Louisville. I would have run them past you first, but you weren't available."

"I'm sure they're fine." Sienna waved a hand. "I'm happy to leave the details to you."

"You need to be at the studio by eight o'clock tomorrow morning," Dirk went on. "They want an hour to do your hair and makeup."

"Great." Her smile was forced as they followed him into the room. "I can hardly wait."

"Mr. Green, if you don't mind, I have a few questions." Zeke decided it was time to take over the trajectory of the conversation.

"Like what?" To his credit, Dirk looked genuinely confused. "I listened to your message but had no idea why anyone from the Milwaukee Police Department would need to speak to me." Sienna's manager spread his hands. "I don't live here and haven't been involved in anything illegal."

"Where you were last night?" Zeke asked. "From eight o'clock to about ten?"

Dirk frowned. "Here at the hotel. I had a late dinner in the restaurant, then headed up to my room." He glanced at Sienna. "The food is amazing; you should try it."

Zeke could only imagine how much Dirk's meal had cost and mentally compared that to the frozen pizza's they'd eaten. From what he knew of Sienna, she'd preferred the grocery store pizza. "Do you have a bill so we can verify that?"

"Um, sure. But I, um, put it on my room." Dirk looked a bit guilty as if knowing the tab would shock Sienna. "I can get a copy from the front desk."

"Great, that works. So you were here all evening?" Zeke pressed.

"Yes, I was on the phone for a few hours making the arrangements for Sienna's interviews." Dirk frowned. "You haven't told me what this is about. Why all the questions?"

"I'll get to that," he answered evasively. "Have you been

in contact with Josh Allenton while you've been here in town?"

"Josh? No." Again, Dirk darted a glance at Sienna. If the guy was acting, he was pretty good. "You mentioned early on that you weren't on good terms with your ex-husband. Why would he call me?"

"To check up on Sienna. Maybe to know what she's been doing," Zeke said. "I need you to be honest with me, Mr. Green. Have you spoken to Josh Allenton either in person or on the phone since you've been in Milwaukee?"

"In person? Isn't he in Los Angeles?" Dirk shook his head. "No, I have not spoken to Josh. I have no reason to. Even if he did try to contact me, I wouldn't call him back." Now his expression turned earnest as he looked at Sienna. "I know that talking to him would upset you. This tour is important to both of us. I would never jeopardize that."

"Allenton is wealthy," Zeke said. "Maybe he paid you to keep him updated on where Sienna was staying and what she was doing."

"I know he's rich, but I haven't spoken to him." Dirk's face flushed with anger. "You want to check my phone?"

"Yes, that would be very helpful," Zeke said.

Dirk's jaw dropped in shock, as if he never expected Zeke to follow through on his offer. Little did Dirk know that a cop never turned down information that was voluntarily offered. Some crooks felt they could outsmart a cop by appearing to cooperate fully, essentially bluffing their way out.

They were wrong.

"Here." Dirk pulled his phone from his pocket and thrust it at him. "You want to look at my call log? Go ahead."

"Thank you." Zeke knew Dirk could have a disposable phone, too, but would start here. "Please unlock it for me."

Dirk's scowl deepened, but he did as Zeke asked, then handed it back. "I'd still like to know what this is about."

"Yes, I know. Would you please go up to the front desk to get that hotel bill while I do this?" Zeke smiled. "Once I verify your actions, we'll be out of your hair."

Dirk glanced at Sienna. "Did something happen? Why are you looking at me as if I'm some sort of criminal?"

Zeke gave her a subtle shake of his head, indicating she shouldn't give anything away.

"I'm concerned about my safety and Bailey's too," Sienna said. "We really appreciate your cooperation."

"Like I have a choice?" Dirk jumped to his feet and stalked to the front desk.

Zeke showed Sienna Dirk's phone screen. "See Josh's number on here?"

She took the phone and scrolled through Dirk's recent calls. After a long moment, she sighed. "No, I don't. But you know he could have a cheap disposable phone on him."

"I'll get to that. What about the other numbers? Any you don't recognize?" Zeke knew Dirk could very well be chatting with someone Josh hired rather than Josh himself. "I plan to take note of the numbers and check them out, but it would be nice if you could help narrow the list."

"Yes, I don't know this one." She pointed at it. Zeke quickly jotted it down. "And there was another one . . . yeah, this one." She turned the screen toward him again so he could make a note of that one too. "Josie from the PR team has this number. Looks like she and Dirk have been in touch a lot."

Maybe Dirk hadn't lied about that. He took the phone and continued double-checking the list of numbers. There was only one that had the local 414 area code. He made a note of that, even though he felt certain it was probably the local TV station.

"Here." Dirk thrust a sheet of paper toward him. "This is my bill to date. You can see the dinner on there."

"Wow, did you order the steak and lobster?" He eyed the staggering amount. "The cost of your meal is a third of my house payment."

Dirk avoided Sienna's gaze without answering. Zeke had to resist the urge to sock the guy in the arm for taking advantage of his position as Sienna's manager.

But it was her job to rein him in, not his. Another thought struck. "What sort of rental car are you driving?"

"A silver Honda Civic." Dirk looked confused again. At least that car was reasonable. He'd half expected the guy to be driving a BMW or Mercedes.

Glancing at the phone, he jotted down two more numbers and then began to call them.

"Wait, what are you doing? You can't call people in my phone." Dirk looked so panicked, he wondered if the guy had called an escort service or something. "That's my business."

"Yes, and I need to make sure you're not speaking to anyone who is connected with Josh Allenton," Zeke said.

"Let me see those numbers," Dirk said, craning his neck to look at Zeke's notepad. "I can tell you who they belong to."

"See, that's the thing. I can't just take your word for it." Zeke smiled again, but Dirk was not seeing the humor in the situation.

"Okay, okay!" Dirk squirmed in his seat for a moment, then said, "I've been offering my manager services to other potential clients. Those numbers belong to Rachel, Christine, and Jonas."

Of course, he was. Zeke noted the flash of anger and hurt in Sienna's gaze, but he jotted the names down and proceeded to call each of them to make sure the names were real.

Surprisingly, they were.

"Do you have another phone?" Zeke asked.

"What? No, why?" It took Dirk a minute to understand. He stood and began emptying his pockets, dumping his wallet, keys, a nail clipper, a pack of gum, and a money clip onto the table. "This is all I have on me."

Zeke reached over to pat his pockets to make sure they were empty. Then he glanced at Sienna and shrugged.

From what he could tell, Dirk Green was telling the truth. The guy might be on the sleazy side, but he wasn't communicating with Josh to set Sienna up for these attacks.

And if not Dirk, then who?

CHAPTER ELEVEN

The fact that Dirk was looking for more clients shouldn't have surprised her, but the news had hit Sienna hard. For the simple reason that she hadn't anticipated he'd do such a thing.

Yet really, could she blame him? The guy deserved to make a name for himself in this business. One client, who wasn't even that big of a deal in the grand scheme of things, wasn't going to sustain him for long.

And that wasn't even taking into consideration the possibility that she'd have to pull out of this tour.

Yet that coupled with how much he'd spent during his time in the city was another blow. The money in her *Sienna!* account was the advance on her tour, with an additional payment being provided after each show. Obviously, this was her fault, as she should have given Dirk a daily allowance. To her shame, it hadn't occurred to her that Dirk would take advantage of their arrangement like this.

Zeke gave her a questioning glance, silently asking if she had anything to add. She didn't, at least as far as the interview regarding Dirk being implicated in the attacks.

But the cost of his room and meals? Oh yeah. She can and would do something about that. She shouldn't have been so foolish to allow this in the first place. At the time, she had only cared about the money she needed to support her and Bailey. She knew Dirk had gotten his cut of the advance, but she'd allowed him to put business expenses on her account.

Not any longer.

She turned to look at Dirk. "I'm closing the *Sienna!* account. Starting from this point forward, you'll be paying for all of this"—she waved at their luxurious surroundings—"out of your own account. Not mine. I will give you an allowance for each day to spend as you like. Be aware, it won't cover the suite here or meals like the one you had last night."

"But . . . you can't . . . ," Dirk sputtered.

"She can," Zeke interjected. "You have been taking advantage of Sienna's kindness. Do you think your other clients are going to give you an open checkbook to live on?" Zeke snorted. "Not likely."

Dirk's face flushed red, and she could tell he wanted nothing more than to unload on her. Apparently, Zeke's presence had him biting his tongue. She sat in silence, waiting for him to get control of himself.

"Fine," Dirk finally said in a clipped tone. "I'll check out today."

"Good." She stood. "We'll do that right now. I'll walk up to the front desk with you so I can get a final bill. That way, the charge won't bounce after I close the account."

Dirk's red face didn't subside, but he didn't argue either. He rose, then said, "I need to pack my things."

"Go ahead. We'll wait," Sienna said.

Dirk muttered something harsh under his breath, then

headed for the elevator. Once he was well out of earshot, she sighed and ran her fingers through her hair. With a grimace, she glanced at Zeke. "I know what you're thinking. I've been a complete and total idiot."

"No, you haven't," he said to her surprise. "Maybe you've been naïve and too trusting, but not a fool. I know that money alone isn't the motivator for what you're doing, Sienna. You're singing your praises to God and sharing your talents with others so they can do the same. Dirk doesn't understand that part of your life."

"No, he doesn't."

"Dirk shouldn't have taken advantage of the situation, and he knows it," Zeke said with a scowl. "I'm glad you stepped up to put an end to that."

She managed a lopsided smile. "Thanks to you being here, that was much easier than I expected. I guess I should fire him, but I don't have the time or energy to find a new manager. And really, depending on how the rest of the day goes, I may not even need one. This . . . might be over before it's started."

Zeke stepped closer, his dark eyes intense. "Don't give up. I know it doesn't seem like much, but we learned a lot today."

"Maybe we did, but I don't see how it helps. If Dirk hasn't been in touch with Josh, then who has been tracking my phone?" She frowned. "Speaking of which, I should have kept the stupid thing long enough to cancel the account. It's going to be difficult to get in without having a phone to verify who I am."

"Hang on, I'll ask Gabe to grab it." Zeke made the call, and she could just imagine the team's tech expert going through the garbage to retrieve her phone. It would have been funny if the situation wasn't so serious.

When finished, Zeke glanced around the ornate lobby. "I don't think there's more to learn here. I guess without another lead we'll head back to the safe house."

As much as she wanted to hug her daughter, the thought of going back with nothing more than what they knew at this moment was depressing. She tried to think of another person who Josh may have used to track her phone and belatedly remembered her ex's college roommate. So much had happened she couldn't recall where things stood on that portion of Zeke's investigation. "What about Brett Voss? Is there anything we can do to find him while we're here?"

Zeke considered that for a moment. "I doubt Voss is staying in a place like this, or anywhere else in the downtown area of the city. I'll check with Gabe to see if he has anything more once we're back in the SUV. I was hoping the BOLO would have yielded some results by now. But I'm sure someone would have called me if that was the case."

"I understand." She spotted Dirk rolling his large suitcase out of the elevator. His expression was surly, but he didn't vent his anger when he caught her gaze. Forcing a smile, she waited for him to approach before turning toward the front desk.

"Checking out?" the clerk asked.

"Yes." Dirk didn't so much as look at her as the desk clerk printed up a final bill and accepted his room key.

"I hope you visit again soon," the woman said with a bright smile.

Don't count on it, Sienna thought. The historic hotel was nice, but there was no way she would be staying there. She waited for Dirk to push the bill toward her, before picking it up and scanning the total.

And nearly gasped out loud.

Seriously? The suite Dirk had been staying in cost $650 per night. And that didn't include taxes, fees, and all the meals he'd placed on the room bill. The house she'd rented in White Gull Bay had been half the cost of the bill she was looking at. And that had housed three people, two adults and one child, for an entire week. This bill was only for the past three days!

This—this was outrageous. But there was no point in rehashing the choices Dirk had made. He knew she was upset, and she'd certainly made her point by forcing him to check out. With a calm deliberation she didn't feel, she folded the folio and tucked it into her pocket. Doing her best to mask her anger, she turned to face him. "Where will you stay for the rest of the week?"

"Why do you care?" Dirk shot back.

Yeah, why did she? It wasn't as if she planned to visit him again. With a shrug, she nodded. "Suit yourself. Take care, Dirk. I'll see you tomorrow morning bright and early for the TV interview." Turning away, she started to walk back to Zeke. He'd stayed behind, likely to give her space for a private conversation with Dirk.

Sweet, but unnecessary.

"Sienna." She paused, glancing back over her shoulder when Dirk called her name. For a moment, she saw genuine concern in his eyes. "You never told me why you and your cop fiancé were asking so many questions. Is there something going on? Are you and Bailey in danger from your ex-husband?"

"Nothing you need to worry about. Take care of yourself. See you soon." She hated lying to him, but Dirk wasn't the one in danger.

Then again, he would suffer a huge setback if she canceled the tour. Drawing in a deep breath, she walked away.

It wouldn't matter to Dirk if she canceled today, tomorrow, or Friday. He'd suffer the same financial blow regardless.

And so would she. The only reason she was at all concerned about that was due to the legals fees that were no doubt piling up with the various motions Josh's attorney was throwing at her.

Enough. Worrying about the legal fees or how she'd support herself if she was forced to abandon her career and disappear wasn't helpful. God would give her the strength and courage she needed.

But today was all about trying to find whoever was helping Josh strike out at her.

And stopping him before she was forced to take drastic measures.

***

ZEKE WATCHED Dirk leave the hotel with a sense of relief. At least the guy wouldn't be a drain on Sienna financially from this point forward.

He wished Dirk had been working for Allenton, but the guy had at least that much decency. Maybe he felt as if he deserved special treatment, despite how the crux of his job was to showcase Sienna.

Not himself.

"Let's go." Zeke caught Sienna's hand in his. "I can't believe I'm saying this, but let's stop and get something to eat. My treat," he quickly added.

"I'm not broke," she protested.

"Maybe not, but I know a great place we can get a fantastic meal at a very reasonable price." He grinned, trying to lighten the mood.

"Is this a place from when we were young?"

"Nope. It's relatively new over the past two years, maybe three." He steered her toward the parking lot across the street. He glimpsed a silver car exiting the same parking lot, and seeing a scowling Dirk Green behind the wheel, he was glad to know the guy hadn't lied about the rental car. He opened the car door for her. "Rosie's Diner is incredible. She's from Ireland and serves fresh bakery each day. You'll love it."

"Sounds good." Her smile didn't quite reach her eyes. There wasn't anything he could do about Dirk, but she was right about one thing. Time was running out.

He needed a lead on Brett Voss, and quick.

As promised, he called Gabe once they were on the road. "Now what?" Gabe demanded. "I can't get anything done with you constantly interrupting me."

"Yeah, sorry about that." Gabe was sounding testier than usual. "Is everything okay?"

There was a brief pause, then Gabe sighed. "Rhy just sent Cassidy and several other members of the team out to an active shooter situation. I get nervous about those types of perps. They don't care how many people they take out before killing themselves."

Ah, so that was it. Gabe was harboring a not-so-secret crush on Cassidy. "Cass is a smart cop, she'll be fine."

"I know." Gabe seemed to realize he was allowing his personal concern to show. "I got Sienna's phone like you asked. What else do you need?"

"Anything on Brett Voss or Josh Allenton." Zeke

checked the rearview mirror but didn't see anything concerning. "We were able to cross Dirk Green off as a suspect. I checked his phone and made him empty his pockets to verify he wasn't carrying a throwaway. I didn't find any evidence he's been in touch with Allenton, which puts us right back at square one."

"Okay, I'll see what I can do," Gabe said. "Before the active shooter call out, I heard Rhy saying something about how Allenton's buddy vouched for him, but that they weren't necessarily convinced the dude wasn't lying."

That was a view he shared, but Zeke didn't mention it. "Sounds good."

"Oh, and Joe got a search warrant for videos of all the gas stations in a five-mile radius of the Wooden Nickel," Gabe continued. "I've been searching for anyone matching Voss or Allenton's photos. I'm hoping one or both of them stopped in at some point."

"That's a good idea." Zeke knew that many people didn't realize how many cameras were in the city. Although someone like Allenton might have thought of that and taken precautions to hide his features. "If you see anyone that looks remotely suspicious, like wearing a hoodie or a hat low to cover his features, let me know. I don't want to rule anyone out until we've had a chance to vet them."

"I will. Is that all? Or do you need something else?" Gabe asked.

"That's good for now, thanks. And I'll say a prayer for Cass."

"Thanks, Zeke."

"What's up with Gabe and Cassidy?" Sienna asked.

"Nothing yet as far as I know." He shrugged. "But give it time. It's no secret Gabe has a crush on her."

"I could tell," Sienna said with a smile.

Zeke checked the rearview mirror, then caught sight of Rosie's sign. The parking lot was only half full, probably because it was midmorning. The breakfast rush was over by now, but he knew from experience there would still be plenty of fresh-baked goods.

After parking and sliding out from behind the wheel, the scent of cinnamon wafted toward him. Rosie's cinnamon rolls were his favorite.

"Something smells good," Sienna said as they went inside.

"Ach, Zeke, 'tis good to see you, lad," Rosie greeted him with enthusiasm. She seemed to have a soft spot for Rhy Finnegan and his siblings and had spread that same good-will to the rest of the tactical team. "And who's this fine lass you've brought to see me?"

"Hi, Rosie, this is Sienna Reynolds. My fiancée," he belatedly remembered to add. "Sienna, I'm thrilled to introduce you to Rosie, the best cook in town."

"It's a pleasure to meet you, Rosie," Sienna said with a smile. "Zeke raves about your breakfasts."

"Ach, lass, the pleasure is mine." Rosie's eyes gleamed as she spied his mother's engagement ring. "How wonderful to hear you and Zeke will be getting married! Come, lass, have a seat. I'll fetch you two of my fresh-baked cinnamon rolls. And would you be wanting coffee too?"

"Yes, please," Sienna said. "The cinnamon rolls sound wonderful."

"They're larger than my head," Zeke joked as they slid into an empty booth. "But delicious all the same."

"I can see why you and your teammates like it here," Sienna said as she glanced around the homey yet modest restaurant. "No fuss, no muss."

"And the best full Irish breakfast you can get in the

country," he said. "No lie, every time I come in here, I'm tempted to book a trip to Ireland."

"Two cinnamon rolls warm from the oven," Rosie declared as she set two of her giant pastries on the table. Then she darted away to fetch their coffee.

"Wow, this is bigger than your head," Sienna said with a laugh. Her eyes widened after she took a bite. "Hmm, the melted icing is amazing."

"Are ya ready to order, then?" Rosie asked, after filling their coffee cups.

"I'll have the full Irish," Zeke said. He leaned forward. "Trust me, you'll love it too."

"Sure, why not? I'll have the full Irish as well," Sienna agreed.

"Ach, I trust you won't be disappointed. Enjoy." With that, Rosie hurried away.

For several minutes, they ate their cinnamon rolls and drank their coffee. Then Sienna rested her elbows on the table. "I'm not sure what to do."

He knew she was talking about her imposed deadline and the plan to disappear rather than to continue fighting Josh's custody battle through the legal system. One that could fail to protect her and Bailey.

"I can't tell you what to do. Other than to give me time to find the proof we need to shut Josh's court filing down for good." Hard to sound confident when he had nothing to go on, other than hoping Josh and his hired gun would make another mistake. "Brett Voss is likely the one involved. I'm sure we can convince him to cooperate."

In a way they had not been able to do with Ken Holt. Although in truth, Holt's murder should help Voss see the light. Unless Voss did the deed.

"I don't have a right to ask you this, but I need to find someone that will make new passports for me and Bailey."

He shook his head. "I don't know anyone with those skills, and if I did, I'd have to arrest them." He hated disappointing her. "I would do a lot to protect you and your daughter. But breaking the law?" He winced. "I don't know that I can cross that line."

"Of course, you can't. I completely understand." Sienna held his gaze. "I would only ask that you don't turn me in. Just let us disappear."

"I won't turn you in, but let's pray right now that it won't come to that." He reached across the table to take her hand. "Lord Jesus, please protect Sienna and Bailey. Hold them close in Your loving arms and grant me the strength and wisdom to find those responsible for trying to hurt them. Amen."

"Amen," Sienna whispered. She clung to his hand for a long time, letting him go only when Rosie brought their heaping plates of food.

"Thanks, Rosie," Zeke said as the sizzling scent teased his senses. "Looks amazing as always."

Sienna murmured her agreement, but while he dug into his meal with gusto, she took small bites, moving food around on her plate more than eating it.

Could he really let her disappear forever? Every cell in his body rejected the idea, but at the same time, he could see why taking that route appealed to Sienna. She had been a victim of Josh's physical abuse. Allowing him to touch a single hair on Bailey's head could not be allowed to happen.

Now his appetite was fading as he considered the day stretching endlessly before them. There had to be a way to break this case open.

Too bad he was out of ideas.

"Aye, lad, can I get you anything else?" Rosie asked, after refilling their cups. Her bright red hair was likely from a bottle, but the twinkle in her eye was real. "Perhaps another cinnamon roll?"

"No, thank you." He patted his lean belly. "Everything was excellent as always, but I'm stuffed."

"Well, then, have a fine day." Rosie slipped the bill under the edge of his plate, then turned to check in on her other customers.

He forced himself to take another bite. When his phone rang, his pulse kicked up when he saw Gabe's name. He quickly answered. "Hey, Gabe. Everything okay?"

"What? Oh yeah, the active shooter was found dead of a self-inflicted gunshot wound to the head. Cass and the others are fine." There was no mistaking the relief in Gabe's tone at knowing Cassidy was safe. "I found something on one of the gas station videos. Like you mentioned, the guy keeps his head down and is wearing a ball cap. His hair is blond, though, and he doesn't look like your dead guy. He pays for gas, then can be seen walking away while talking on the phone."

"Any chance you can zoom in on the video to see if you can figure out who he might be talking to?"

"Nah, that's impossible as he has the phone up to his face. But I got a license plate number and a corresponding address and registration."

Now they were talking. "A black car? Who is it registered to?"

"It is a black Dodge Hornet, a smaller SUV," Gave said. "And it's registered to a guy named Toby Belinsky."

The name meant nothing to him. "Toby Belinsky?" he

repeated, glancing at Sienna. She frowned and shook her head, indicating she didn't recognize the name. "Is Belinsky from California?" If only they could be so fortunate.

"Nah, he's from Wisconsin, here in the Milwaukee area," Gabe said. "I have an address for his house in Timberland Falls."

Of course, it had to be Timberland Falls where the cops did not appreciate the members of the tactical team. Several times Rhy had to pull rank to take over a case that had happened in their jurisdiction. But Zeke didn't care, they had a lead, and that was all that mattered. He wasn't going to let the Timberland Falls PD keep him from following the trail that could lead to Allenton. "Great. Give me the address."

Gabe rattled it off. It was one of those really long addresses with north this and west that, which sometimes wreaked havoc with GPS systems, but he'd find it.

"Thanks so much. Do you know anything else about this guy? Does he have a criminal record?"

"Hang on." Gabe tapped a few keys. "No—well, he does have a financial judgment against him from five years ago but nothing more recent. Do you want me to dig into the particulars?"

Financial judgments were typically an indication of cash flow problems. But it was hard to imagine something from five years ago would cause Toby Belinsky to cross the line into becoming a criminal now.

But it was still worth checking out.

"Yes please, thanks, Gabe. I'll head over there ASAP." He dug money from his wallet and left cash on the table, along with a generous tip. "Call me if you find anything else."

"Will do. Later." Gabe ended the call.

"Where are we going?" Sienna asked.

He hesitated, remembering the last time he went against his better judgment by bringing her along to interview a witness. That had ended badly.

Not that Holt's murder was Sienna's fault. In truth, even if Sienna hadn't been there, the guy might have made the same panicked call to whoever hired him and ended up just as dead.

Yet dropping her off at the safe house would take time. Now that he had an address, he was anxious to hit the road. He could park a distance away from the house, leave Sienna in the car and approach on foot.

The only good news was that the active shooter situation was resolved, so he could possibly get someone from the team to back him up.

"Timberland Falls." He slid out of the booth giving her a hand. "I'll need you to stay in the car this time, though. No argument," he added firmly. "Otherwise, I'll take the time to drop you off with Flynn, Taylor, and Bailey."

"I'll wait in the car." Her voice was subdued, no doubt she was also remembering how things had gone south at the Wooden Nickel.

Minutes later, he was on the road heading north. Cassidy didn't answer, but Grayson did. "What's up?"

"Can you meet me in Timberland Falls? I have a suspect."

"Right away. Give me the address."

Zeke thanked God for the men and women he worked with. He gave the address and briefed Grayson on the situation. "This could be nothing, but the guy appeared to be avoiding the cameras."

"Understood. Can't hurt to have a chat," Grayson agreed.

Sienna was quiet as he drove. He wanted to reassure her that Toby Belinsky was a viable lead.

But all they had was a picture from a gas station where the guy seems to be avoiding the camera.

For all he knew, the guy could be nothing but another dead end.

CHAPTER TWELVE

Sienna's mind didn't register the scenery passing her window. Her thoughts whirled. While she'd thoroughly enjoyed their brief respite of eating at Rosie's Diner, especially hearing Zeke introduce her as his fiancée, now the oppressive weight of her unknown future hovered over her.

Stay or go?

The words bounced in her mind like a Ping-Pong ball darting from one side of the table to the other. Stay? Go? Stay? Go? Stay? Go?

Stop it! She pressed her fingertips to her temples as if she could reach inside her head and pluck the words out. Stressing out about this wasn't helpful. She needed to believe God would send her a clear message as to the path she should take.

When it was time.

"Sienna? Are you okay? Do you have a headache?" Zeke's concerned tone helped steady her nerves. "I can turn around and take you back to the safe house."

"No." The word came out stronger than she'd meant it to. "I mean, I'm fine. Maybe a little tired." That wasn't exactly true. Caffeine zipped through her blood stream at the speed of light.

"If you're sure." Zeke's tone was full of doubt.

"I'm positive." She forced a smile and concentrated on the upcoming interview. "Do you think this Toby Belinsky will cooperate with you?"

"I hope so." Zeke didn't look concerned. "Gabe will continue to dig into his past, see if there's anything we can use as leverage to help convince him to come clean." There was a brief pause, then Zeke added, "To be fair, we don't have proof that he is involved in the attacks against you. He could just clam up and tell us nothing."

"I understand."

Zeke seemed to straighten in his seat when they passed a sign indicating they'd entered Timberland Falls. She hadn't spent much time in the suburb while she'd lived here, but the homes seemed to be well maintained with plenty of trees with leaves just starting to turn orange and yellow and bushes dotting the yards. She had gotten used to the lack of greenery in California; LA was mostly desert. There were pretty palm trees and some bushes, but nothing as beautiful as here.

Home. The word flashed in her mind. She hadn't lived here in seven years, but it was still home.

And maybe it always would be.

"Okay, that's the house," Zeke interrupted her thoughts. She quickly looked where he'd indicated. The plain brown-brick ranch-style home was one of the older homes on the block.

"I see it." Also in contrast to LA, the houses here were spread out from each other on lots that appeared to be at least a half-acre or more, rather than being built practically on top of each other. Land was a premium in California, and the only homes on large lots went for multiple millions of dollars. "I don't see a car in the driveway."

"No, but it could be in the garage. We're looking for a black Dodge Hornet." At her blank look, he added, "It's a small SUV."

"Okay. Maybe this guy is at work?" She frowned as Zeke drove around the block. "You might have asked Grayson to meet you here for nothing."

"We'll find out." He shrugged, then shifted into park. Then he pointed toward his driver's side window. "See that brown brick beyond the white house we're parked in front of? That's the property. I'm letting you know in case you need to get out of here."

Her stomach clenched as he pulled the car key fob from his pocket and handed it over. She hoped her voice didn't betray her fear as she asked, "How long should I sit here and wait for you?"

"I don't know. But you have your disposable phone, right?" When she nodded and pulled it from her pocket, he smiled. "Good. I'll let you know via text messages how things are going."

"Okay." She told herself it was broad daylight and that there was no reason to be concerned. Still, she tucked the key fob into her pocket and dropped the disposable cell phone in the cupholder.

Zeke's expression turned serious. "I want you to wait in the driver's seat. If you hear anything that sounds like gunfire, you need to get out of here as soon as possible."

As there had already been one episode of gunfire since Ken Holt's death, she knew Zeke was prepared for the worst. That they might find this Toby Belinsky guy armed and ready for battle.

"Sienna?" Zeke scowled. "I'm serious about this. Promise me you'll drive away the instant you hear gunfire."

"I promise." She pushed the words past her tight throat. Leaving Zeke behind wouldn't be easy, but she wasn't armed and wouldn't be able to back him up. Much like last night, she was afraid she'd only make things worse if she tried to rush in to save him. "But I need you to promise me something too."

"Like what?"

"That you won't take any unnecessary risks." She reached for his hand, gripping it tightly. "I don't want anything bad to happen to you."

He frowned. "I'm not planning to be reckless. I'm a good cop. However, you need to know that every situation has the potential to go sideways."

"I get that." She tried to offer a reassuring smile. "I just want you back in one piece."

"I'll be fine." Confidence oozed from his tone. "And Grayson will be here any minute." As if his colleague had heard them talking, Zeke's phone rang. "This is him now. Hey, Grayson. We're parked on the next block behind the target house."

There was a pause as Zeke listened.

"Yep, see you soon." Zeke lowered the phone, and a moment later, she saw another black SUV come around the corner and head toward them. The driver was a blond-haired guy who made a Y-turn, then pulled in to park behind them. Zeke glanced at her. "Get behind the wheel so you can be ready to go if needed."

She nodded and pushed out of the car. Grayson joined Zeke, then turned to smile at her. "Congrats! I'm thrilled for you and Zeke."

"Thanks." She returned his smile, then stepped forward

to give Zeke a quick hug. "Be safe, Zeke. I love you." The words came naturally, but she could tell the declaration had caught him off guard.

"I will. Love you too." He gave her a quick kiss, then released her. He turned to Grayson. "I didn't see any sign of movement when I drove by, did you?"

"Nope. I figure we should check the garage first, see if the black Dodge Hornet is in there," Grayson said. He gestured to the house tucked behind the one they were standing in front of. "I think the garage has a side window."

"Great. Oh, by the way, Gabe sent me a copy of this guy's driver's license photo." He held up his phone to show Grayson an image of an unsmiling man. Then Zeke turned the phone so she could see it too. "Does he look familiar?" Zeke asked.

She stared at the picture for a long moment. "No, sorry. If he's a friend of Josh's, I never met him."

"That's fine. I wanted to make sure." Zeke pocketed his phone. Then he shot her a questioning glance. "You'll be okay?"

"Yes, of course." She took that as her cue to get back into the SUV. She slid into the driver's seat, took a moment to adjust the seat, then closed the door. Slouching down in the seat so as not to attract too much attention, she watched as Zeke and Grayson split up and approached the back of the home from two different directions.

It didn't take long for them to disappear from her line of sight. Leaving her little choice but to settle in and wait.

And pray.

ZEKE HAD to take a moment to shake off the impact of Sienna's words.

I love you.

He'd been able to return the sentiment easily enough because it was true. He did love her. With his entire heart.

And that was a problem. Because the more he thought about her leaving town never to be heard from again, the more he wanted to drop off the face of the earth with her.

Throwing his career away in one fell swoop.

That wasn't something he should be thinking of now, though. He cleared his mind and scanned the area. The neighborhood was quiet, maybe because it was noon on Wednesday. There was no sign of anyone at home, but he pressed himself against the brick anyway.

Listening intently, he watched as Grayson took the opposite side of the home. His teammate paused, peeked in through the garage window, then turned away. Grayson caught Zeke's gaze and shook his head.

Great. No car probably meant Toby Belinsky wasn't home. Still, he intended to make sure. Belinsky could have left the SUV somewhere and taken a rideshare home.

Especially if he had gone out drinking after killing a guy.

Then again, someone in a black SUV had taken shots at Sienna outside the seventh district police station. So maybe Belinsky was still out and about, trying to track Sienna's phone again.

He nodded at Grayson to indicate he understood, then edged to the closest window. There were no blinds covering the opening, so he could easily see into what appeared to be a junk room. Maybe once an office but the desk could barely be seen beyond the stacks of papers and boxes piled on top. There were other boxes along the walls, as if

Belinsky had moved in recently but hadn't gotten around to unpacking.

He should have asked Gabe to run down the list of property owners to understand when Belinsky may have purchased the place. After finding nothing interesting in the junk room, he moved on to the next window.

This one did have drapes. There was a small gap, but it was hard to see into the room beyond. He could just make out the mattress and headboard, but that was it. The bed was unmade though, so likely the primary bedroom.

The guy wasn't sleeping it off. Still, he continued moving until he'd checked the next window, the clouded glass identifying it as a bathroom, and the next, which was a messy living room.

Grayson was doing the same thing, peering into the windows until they were able to meet up near the garage.

"See anyone?" Zeke whispered.

"Negative. You?"

Zeke shook his head. "I couldn't really see into the bathroom, but I'm convinced the place is empty."

"Agree. Our target isn't home," Grayson murmured.

Zeke frowned, glancing around the spacious backyard. There was a concrete slab that could be used as a patio, but no outdoor furniture. That in addition to all the boxes made him think Belinsky hadn't lived there long.

"What are you thinking?" Grayson asked.

"Give me a minute to reach out to Gabe." He really wanted to know if this guy had moved in recently. He considered using a text, then decided it would be easier to talk it through over the phone.

"What's up, Zeke? Find something?" Gabe asked.

"We're at the Belinsky residence now." Zeke kept his voice low. "I'm seeing a lot of boxes inside and am curious how long this guy has lived here." If Belinsky was new to the area, it was less likely he was a part of this. He couldn't imagine that Allenton had bought the place for the gunman.

"Sure, that information is publicly accessible." Gabe's fingers clattered on the keyboard. "This is how real estate agents reach out to homeowners to see if they're interested in selling their home."

Zeke was familiar with the practice; he'd gotten those postcard flyers too. The real estate market was hot these days. He continued scanning the area as he waited for Gabe.

"Okay, it looks like Belinsky has been living there for two years. The previous owner was also a Belinsky, though. A Louise Belinsky. Looks as if he paid less than market value for the property. Maybe Louise is his mother, grand-mother, or aunt, and she chose to sell it to him for a discounted price. I'll have to dig deeper if you want that information."

That was interesting. "Yes, please do dig deeper into who Louise Belinsky is and her relationship to Toby," Zeke said. "I appreciate your help on this."

"Anytime," Gabe said. "I'll let you know what I find out."

"Later." He lowered the phone and quickly filled Grayson in on the information. "I inherited my mother's house when she died. Could be a similar situation here."

"Maybe. Let's hope he didn't kill dear old Louise and hide her body in the freezer," Grayson said with a sigh.

Zeke knew Grayson meant it as a joke, but it was a horrible discovery they'd stumbled upon eighteen months ago. A young man had killed his father, stuffed his body in the freezer, then kept his phone so that he could pretend the old man was still alive. The gig was up, though, when the guy's son tried to collect his father's life insurance policy.

No one ever said criminals were smart.

"We'll see what Gabe comes up with. If Louise died or disappeared, he'll let us know." Zeke sighed. "What do you think? I'm torn between going up to knock at the front door and staying back here to wait for Belinsky to return."

"I vote for option number two," Grayson said. "If this guy was here, one of us would have seen him."

"Okay. We'll hang around." Zeke hoped they wouldn't end up wasting an entire day on what could very well prove to be a wild goose chase. "Staying out here might alert the nosy neighbors, so we should park on opposite sides of the street and keep an eye on the place from there."

"I can get on board with that plan. I can even go one block over since we know he's driving a black Dodge Hornet." Grayson grinned. "They're kinda squat and boxy in shape. Should be an easy car to spot."

"Exactly. Here, I'll send you the driver's license photo." He texted Grayson the picture Gabe had provided. Then he quickly texted Sienna. *Heading back to you.*

She responded instantly. *Good.*

Just then he heard the unmistakable sound of a garage door opening. He quickly grabbed Grayson's arm.

"I hear it," Grayson whispered.

He sent another quick text to Sienna. *Wait. Back to original plan. TB is home.*

Her response came two seconds later. *Be careful.*

He wanted to send a heart emoji but stopped himself. There would be time to sort out his feelings later.

Shoving the phone into his pocket, he turned to Grayson. "Let's split up."

Grayson nodded and pointed to the right-hand side of

the ranch home. Zeke quickly turned and moved to the left, anxious to get a glimpse of Belinsky driving in. As he reached the left front corner, he saw a black car slowing as it approached the driveway. Then as if watching in slow motion, the vehicle turned into the driveway.

A Dodge Hornet just as Gabe had told them.

With his back pressed against the wall, he considered how to approach their target. Zeke didn't want to lose this guy, similar to how Ken Holt had fled from the Wooden Nickel. Yet they needed to interview him.

A direct approach seemed the best option. He sent a text to Grayson. *I'm going to knock at the front door. Cover the back.*

Grayson's reply was the okay sign.

Zeke listened as a car door opened and closed. The garage door closed, too, and after another full minute passed, he figured Toby Belinsky was inside the house.

He sent Grayson another text. *Heading up now. Stay alert.*

Got it.

Zeke waited another minute, then walked down to the street. From there, he walked along the road until he reached the driveway. Pretending as if he'd parked a car down the street, he strode up the driveway and then along the uneven sidewalk to the front door, the way any other normal person would.

After pulling his badge from his pocket, he boldly knocked at the front door.

For a long moment, he only heard silence. If he hadn't heard and seen Belinsky come home, he'd assume there was nobody inside. He knocked a second time.

The front door swung open, revealing a scowling man

that sort of resembled the driver's license photo. Although this guy looked older and gaunt.

Maybe the life of crime didn't agree with him.

He also wore a hoodie, much like Gabe had described from the gas station video.

"No solicitation," Belinsky said in a rude, loud voice. He glared at Zeke through the screen door, then stepped back as if to slam the door shut.

"I'm a cop." Zeke held up his badge. "Officer Hawthorne with the Milwaukee Police Department. Are you Mr. Toby Belinsky? I need to ask you a few questions."

Even through the screen, he saw Belinsky's eyes widen with horror. Then the guy shrank from him as if he were a rattlesnake, and he was afraid of being bitten. Without uttering another word, he abruptly slammed the door shut.

Well now, that wasn't very polite.

This was not the response he'd hoped for, but he wasn't about to let this guy off so easy. He pounded on the door again. "Mr. Belinsky?" He raised his voice loud enough that Grayson and any neighbor with an open window could hear him. "Police! I need you to open the door so I can ask you a few questions!"

Apparently, Toby Belinsky was not interested in cooperating. Which made him think they might have the right guy. Most law-abiding citizens didn't slam the door when a cop showed up on their doorstep.

After another long ten seconds of silence, he pounded and shouted again, mentally braced for a violent response.

He was about to text Grayson a warning when he heard his teammate shout, "Stop! Police!"

Then he heard the sharp report of gunfire.

No! Pulling his weapon, Zeke sprinted to the left, knowing

Grayson was somewhere along the right side of the brick home. He took the corner so tight he scraped his arm along the ancient brick, then headed full-bore into the backyard.

Another crack of gunfire had his heart jumping into his throat. Was Grayson hurt?

Dead?

Fearing the worst, he entered the backyard, stopping short when he saw Belinsky lying on the ground, his hand resting on his chest. Grayson was bending over him, and from what Zeke could tell, his fellow teammate wasn't injured.

"He bolted out the door, then turned to take a shot at me," Grayson said, his expression grim. "I had little choice but to return fire."

"I heard. It's not your fault." He pulled out his phone and dialed 911, requesting officers and an ambulance on scene. Then he knelt beside the fallen man. "Are you Toby Belinsky?"

The injured man didn't answer, but up close the resemblance to the driver's license was spot-on. Seeing the blood pooling on Belinsky's chest had him grabbing fistfuls of the guy's hoodie sweatshirt and pressing down on the wound.

"Come on, Toby, talk to me," Zeke said, willing the injured man to look at him. "Why did you shoot Officer Clark?"

Still no answer. He leaned on the wound, adding his weight as pressure. That made Belinsky groan, sweat popping out on his forehead. It seemed to Zeke's nonmedical eye that the guy was growing pale with each passing second. He did not want this man to die, yet he also knew it wasn't at all likely Belinsky would survive a point-blank bullet wound to the chest.

They needed to get him to talk!

"Did you fire shots at Sienna Reynolds?" He could see Grayson was bagging Belinsky's weapon as evidence. The gun might well answer the question of whether he shot at Sienna, so he moved on. "Did someone hire you to stalk Sienna? To try to scare her? Hurt her? Kill her?"

Belinsky's eyelids fluttered open, as if just now realizing Zeke was talking to him. His eyes were shadowed with confusion.

He was going into shock from blood loss.

"Please tell us who hired you." Zeke was well aware he was practically begging now. "Did you know that someone murdered Ken Holt? Was that you?"

The name didn't seem to register. Maybe Belinsky didn't know the guy's name.

If Belinsky hadn't fired first, he'd be afraid they'd shot the wrong man.

Finally, Belinsky moved his lips as if he were going to tell him what he needed to know. "Save me."

"I am. I'm holding pressure on your wound, and the ambulance will be here any second." He did his best to sound confident and reassuring. "Tell me who hired you. I know you didn't do any of this on your own."

Belinsky groaned again, his eyes drifting to the right.

"Come on, Toby." It was all Zeke could do not to shake the guy by the shoulders. "Talk to me! Who hired you?"

"Al . . ." Belinsky's voice faded, and his eyes slid closed.

"Who hired you?" Zeke repeated. "Josh Allenton? Is that what you were trying to say?"

Belinsky didn't respond, his entire body going limp.

"Grayson, check for a pulse." Zeke didn't let up on the double-fisted pressure he was leveraging on the chest wound. As Grayson put his hand to the man's neck to search for a carotid pulse, he prayed Belinsky wouldn't die.

Then Grayson grimaced and shook his head.

A wave of helplessness washed over him. Zeke's chin dropped to his chest as the wail of sirens filled the air. It was too late. He didn't even care if he had to face off with the less than friendly Timberland Falls Police Department.

Toby Belinsky was dead.

Had Toby really implicated Josh Allenton?

He thought so. But that didn't mean they were any closer to finding the proof they needed that Josh Allenton had hired Belinsky to go after Sienna.

CHAPTER THIRTEEN

Drive away. She was supposed to drive away!

She couldn't. Well, she did follow Zeke's instructions to a certain extent. She pulled away from the curb when the distinct sound of gunfire reached her ears, but she only drove around the block.

Craning her neck, she scanned the front of the brick house as she passed by. She didn't see anyone, so she knew the gunfire must have come from the backyard.

Heart in her throat, she ended up right where she'd started, in front of the white house that butted up against Belinsky's home. The angle was such that she couldn't see enough of Toby's backyard. Worrying her lower lip, she considered her options. Stay within the relative safety of the car or get out to find Zeke.

What if he was down? Bleeding from a gunshot wound? She couldn't stand sitting there without knowing if Zeke was hurt.

Or worse.

She glanced at her phone, but of course, there was no

message. Nothing since the one that instructed her to wait because Toby Belinsky had come home.

She killed the engine and pushed the driver's side door open. That's when she heard Zeke's voice.

"Who hired you? Tell us who hired you?"

After a wave of relief at hearing Zeke interrogating the suspect, she moved forward. Was this it? The moment they'd know for certain her ex-husband had hired Belinsky to follow and attack her?

"Talk to me!" Zeke's tone grew desperate. "Talk to me!"

The wailing of sirens indicated the local police were on their way. Feeling better about her decision not to leave, Sienna hurried forward.

"Zeke?" She gasped when she saw that Zeke and Grayson were crouched over the fallen man. Despite her calling Zeke's name, neither man paid any attention to her.

"No pulse," Grayson said. "Start chest compressions."

Zeke's expression was grave as he began to administer chest compressions. His hands were awash with blood as he pressed Belinsky's chest down.

Even from where she stood, she knew their efforts weren't going to help. Toby's features were slack, and he didn't respond to the painful thrusts on his chest. But she also knew they wouldn't stop.

Shaking off her inertia, she rushed forward. "What can I do to help?"

Zeke flashed her an annoyed glance but didn't say anything other than counting his chest compressions out loud. Grayson was doing his best to hold Toby's airway open. She knew from learning CPR after having Bailey that mouth-to-mouth breathing was no longer required. Holding the airway open while chest compressions were performed was all that was needed.

"What's going on?" Two uniformed officers came around the corner of the brick house. Sienna moved away so that Zeke and Grayson could fill them in.

"We announced ourselves as police officers and tried to ask a few questions," Grayson said as Zeke continued to provide chest compressions. "He bolted out the back door. When I shouted at him to stop, he turned and fired a gun at me. I ducked and returned fire, striking him in the chest."

The older cop's eyes narrowed. "Are you from that Milwaukee tactical team? Working under a Rhyland Finnegan?"

"Yes." Grayson reached over and picked up a bag. "This is his gun. I'd like to take it to our lab for processing. Oh, and I have his cell phone here too. I took it from his pocket."

"Here we go again," the older guy muttered harshly. "You're stomping right over our crime scene and horning in on our case."

"Look, we didn't expect this guy to bolt or fire a gun," Grayson said with annoyance. "All we wanted was to ask a few questions."

"Well, it looks to me like you're not getting any answers." The younger cop jerked his thumb toward the victim Zeke was giving chest compressions to. "He's not talking."

Zeke and Grayson had mentioned the possible animosity they'd face by coming here, but Sienna couldn't believe the Timberland Falls cops' attitudes. As if this was somehow their fault.

Just then, two paramedics came into view, pushing a gurney topped with medical equipment over the bumpy lawn. Zeke continued to provide chest compressions as the two first responders began connecting equipment to the fallen man. Then they nudged him aside so they could examine the victim.

"Wait a minute, he has a gunshot wound to his chest?" one of them said incredulously.

"Yes. Shot at close range," Grayson confirmed.

"I'm going to call this," the other paramedic said. "CPR won't work if his heart has been shredded by a bullet."

"We need him alive," Zeke said, grabbing several cleaning wipes from their medical bag to rid his hands of Belinsky's blood.

"Sorry, but we're not miracle workers," the first paramedic said. "There's no way he'll survive this. Compressing his heart is only going to cause him to lose more blood. I'll talk to the doc at the local hospital, but if he agrees, we're going to call it. Time of death at 1235 p.m."

Zeke closed his eyes for a moment in a gesture of defeat before looking at her. He looked apologetic as he rose to his feet.

"Wait a minute. I remember you," the older cop said.

"Yeah, I remember you too," Zeke shot back. "We'll give you our statements, then we need to get out of here."

"Not so fast, we're not giving this case up to your captain this time," the older cop said with a snarl. "You're on our turf. Again!"

Sienna watched uneasily as the four cops faced off with each other. Zeke looked angry in a way she'd never seen before. His hands curled into fists, and she almost cried out a warning, fearing he was about to punch the Timberland Falls cop.

But he didn't. Instead, he blew out a breath and took a step back. Unclenching his hands, he faced his fellow officers with a calm expression. "We'll have our captain talk to yours. In the meantime, we need a search warrant to go through this guy's house and his phone records. Computer, too, if he has one."

"What exactly are you looking for?" the younger Timberland Falls cop asked.

"We have reason to believe Toby Belinsky was hired to attack Sienna Reynolds." Zeke gestured to her.

She stepped forward, offering a smile. "I'm Sienna, I have a two-year-old daughter, Bailey, and my ex-husband is Josh Allenton. Josh has a history of physical abuse, and I currently have sole custody of our daughter. But he is now fighting for joint custody, and I'm afraid he's trying to scare me into cooperating with him."

"Scare you how?" the younger cop asked. All hint of his previous animosity toward Zeke and Grayson seemed to have vanished. She was glad the officer seemed more concerned about the real crime here, not a battle over turf.

"It started with threatening anonymous notes but has escalated to several shooting attempts, the most recent taking place in Milwaukee while Zeke, er, Officer Hawthorne and I were in the parking lot of the seventh district police station."

The tension between the foursome eased. Maybe it was God's calming hand or the fact that none of the four men liked knowing a woman and child were in danger, but the older cop turned to look at Toby Belinsky who was being strapped onto the gurney. There was no medical equipment connected to him. As she watched, the paramedic pulled the sheet up to cover his face. The doc must have agreed that CPR was useless. "And you think that dirtbag ex-husband of yours hired this guy to shoot you?"

"Yes, that was our working theory," Zeke said. He sighed and rubbed the back of his neck with one hand. "Truth is, we didn't have any hard evidence against Belinsky, just a video of him visiting a gas station near the scene of the crime. I wasn't surprised he slammed the door in my face, but I had Grayson covering the back. I thought he might run, but I did not expect him to shoot at my partner. Under those circumstances, any cop would have returned fire."

There was a long moment as the two officers looked at each other. Finally, the older one grimaced. "Okay, I get it. I wouldn't be happy about a shooting going down outside the police station either. It would have been nice if you'd called us about your intent to interview this guy, though."

Grayson nodded. "You're right, we should have. But when we got here, he wasn't home. No car in the garage, no one inside that we could see. We were about to leave when he pulled up. At that point?" He shrugged. "We didn't want to lose the opportunity."

It looked as if Zeke wanted to say something, but one look from Grayson had him closing his mouth.

There was another moment of silence. "Okay, we need to get the crime scene techs here to find the slugs," the older Timberland Falls officer said. "But if we find them, we'll want to match them with the gun."

This time, Zeke didn't hold his tongue. "After that last situation that unraveled here in your jurisdiction, we shared all the evidence with you and your DA's office. And we were able to turn the ballistics report around relatively quickly too."

"Yeah," Grayson said. "We're not trying to steal your collar. He's dead anyway, right? If you could just allow us to take the slugs and the weapon to our lab, I promise we'll share everything with your team."

"Please," Sienna said, injecting herself into the conversation. "I really need to know if that man was hired by my ex-husband to shoot me. I can't bear the thought of losing the custody hearing. If Josh hurts Bailey. . ." Her voice trailed off.

"Okay, okay." The older cop threw up his hands. "We'll handle this as a joint investigation. Give me a minute to get that search warrant."

"Thank you." She relaxed when Zeke and Grayson turned toward the house.

Now that the danger was over, she couldn't help but wonder how long it would take for the officers to find evidence linking Josh to Toby Belinsky.

An hour? The rest of the day? By morning?

She'd be satisfied with any of the options. As long as it was enough to put Josh away for the rest of his life.

Maybe she wouldn't have to find a way to buy fake passports after all.

ZEKE WAS NOT happy that Sienna hadn't followed his instructions as she'd promised. But it was hard to stay angry when she'd managed to pull off a truce with the Timberland Falls Police Department.

A feat he hadn't thought possible.

He was fairly certain her stunning beauty and charm had been the deciding factor. Well, that and the way her voice had trembled when she'd explained about her ex-husband's physical abuse and the shooting outside the precinct.

Maybe this truce wouldn't last long, but he planned to take advantage of the opportunity to see what was inside Belinsky's home.

Hopefully not Louise in a freezer, but rather phone

records, bank records, or other evidence that Belinsky had been hired by Allenton.

Zeke was convinced the name of Sienna's ex was what Belinsky had tried to say. That he'd been hired by Allenton. What else could he have meant by uttering the syllable *al*?

Now he had to hope and pray they could find the paper trail they needed to prove it. This would have been easier if Belinsky hadn't died, but he couldn't change that outcome. He'd done his best to keep him alive.

He tugged Sienna's arm, pulling her off to the side of the crime scene. "I'm going to ask one of my teammates to head out here so you can get back to the safe house."

"I'm fine waiting here," she said. "I'm sure you'll get the search warrant, right?"

"I don't see why the judge wouldn't grant it, but you can't just sit here and wait. This could easily take hours." He hesitated, then asked, "You weren't planning to do a rehearsal tonight, were you?"

"That was my original plan, but I don't really need to. Unless you tell me the danger is over for good." She frowned. "I don't want to leave you and Grayson. I'll go crazy sitting around the safe house wondering about what's going on."

"You'll go even more crazy sitting around here with nothing to do," he argued. "Trust me on this. Spend some time with your daughter. Maybe go over your play list or something. Leave the police work to us."

She didn't look happy, but he wasn't backing down on this.

"Please, Sienna." He took both of her hands in his. "You didn't drive away at the sound of gunfire like you promised. Please do this for me."

"I did drive away," she said. "I went around the block,

and when I didn't see anything out front, I returned to the original parking spot. I heard you talking to him, so that's why I came to find you."

"That wasn't part of the deal."

"I know." She grimaced. "I couldn't leave. Not when I thought you were the one who'd been shot."

It was nice to know she'd cared enough to rush over. Yet if he had been shot, Belinsky could have gone after her too. For now, he decided not to push the issue of what she should have done.

He needed her to cooperate with him on heading back to the safe house.

Sienna glanced around at the scene. It might look chaotic to a civilian, but he was glad to see how the Timberland Falls officers were placing small evidence markers on key areas, like the blood stain on the ground where Belinsky had fallen. And it also looked as if Grayson was showing them where he'd found the guy's gun.

"Okay, I'll go back." Sienna's expression was resigned. She gently squeezed his hands. "I need you to call me the minute you find any evidence that Belinsky communicated with Josh. I won't be able to relax until I know."

"I will absolutely tell you the moment I find any connection between them." He tugged her closer, then released her hands so he could wrap her into a hug. "I'm sorry Belinsky died, but we'll get to the bottom of this."

"I know." She rested her head on his shoulder for a moment before stepping back. "You have a job to do, so I won't keep you. Make your call. I'll wait in the SUV."

He pulled out his phone and called Rhy. After filling his boss in on the sequence of events that had unfolded in Timberland Falls, he asked, "Is there someone that can head out here to take Sienna back to the safe house?"

"Cassidy was just leaving, hang on a minute." There was a pause as Rhy had a muffled conversation that he couldn't hear. Then his boss returned to the call. "Cass is on her way."

"Great, have her get the address from Gabe. He was digging into Belinsky's background for me too."

"I'll check in with him, but it sounds like you'll have better luck with the search warrant," Rhy said. "Cassidy should be there in fifteen to twenty minutes."

"I'll let Sienna know. Thanks, Rhy." He lowered his phone. "Cassidy is on her way. Why don't you drive the SUV around front? It will be easier for Cass to find you there. Leave the keys in the cupholder. No one will steal it while the squads are parked outside."

"I will." She held his gaze for a moment, then surprised him by stepping in for a brief but sizzling kiss. "I'm glad you're not hurt," she added, before turning away.

He wanted to call her back, to tell her how much he loved her, but didn't. This wasn't the time or the place to discuss his feelings for her.

Evidence first, he reminded himself. He turned and walked over to where Grayson was describing for the third time how Belinsky had bolted out of the back door, turned, then fired at him.

The crime scene techs arrived a few minutes later. Zeke was itching to get into the house but spent some time looking for the slug that had missed Grayson. To his surprise, he found it embedded in a large oak tree.

"Here's the slug," he announced.

"Good eye," Grayson said, coming over to join him. His teammate's expression sobered as he realized the slug was at the same level as his head. "I don't think I should tell Eve how close I came to being hit."

Dr. Eve Shaw-Clark was Grayson's wife and a microbiologist specializing on finding a cure for diabetes.

"That's up to you. Women seem to have a way of finding out things, though." He gave Grayson a one-armed brotherly hug, then turned as the older cop, an Officer Alexander, crossed over to them.

"Got the search warrant." He lifted his phone. It was nice in this age of technology that paperwork could be expedited through email. "Let's head inside."

Zeke was more than ready to follow his Timberland Falls brothers in blue into the home of Toby Belinsky. The back door he'd bolted from was not locked, so that was how they entered. Zeke had to smile when Grayson headed straight for the freezer that was too small for an adult woman's body.

Thankfully, Louise wasn't inside.

Zeke moved through the house quickly, searching for a computer. There wasn't one. He turned to Grayson. "We'll need to get a rush on those phone records."

"Yeah, I will," Grayson agreed. "But we still need to look around. Belinsky could have jotted a few notes down as he talked to Allenton."

Anything was possible. He donned gloves offered by Officer Alexander, then began searching the primary bedroom. To his dismay, there wasn't a single note or slip of paper to be found in the main bedroom. Just the usual assortment of clothing.

When he found a brown uniform hanging in the closet, he paused. Belinsky must have worked as a truck driver delivering packages at some point. He pulled out his phone to call Gabe. "Hey, was Belinsky a delivery driver?"

"Yes, still employed from what I can tell. Why?"

"I found his uniform in the closet. Can you find his

boss? I'll need to interview him to find out his schedule." Zeke felt a glimmer of hope that he'd learn Belinsky had been off for the past two days.

"Anything else," Gabe asked.

"I'm not sure, so keep your phone handy. Thanks." He pocketed the phone and continued to search. Finding nothing unusual, he headed into the bathroom.

And found nothing of interest there either.

Battling frustration, he joined Grayson and the Timberland Falls officers in the main part of the house. "Get anything?" he asked.

"Nothing." Grayson scowled. "Not even the smallest slip of paper. Who doesn't have sticky notes?"

"I think your wife has bought all the ones available within the entire metropolitan area," Zeke joked. Eve was known to have packs upon packs of sticky notes. "Belinsky is a package delivery driver. Gabe is going to shoot me his boss's name and number so we can talk to him."

"Yeah, that might help," Grayson said. "I'm not seeing anything useful here."

The execution of the search warrant was depressingly futile.

"I found his stash of bullets," Officer Alexander said. He lifted the box for them to see. "This should help us match the slug that was taken out of the tree."

The one that had been embedded at the same level as Grayson's head.

A sense of urgency washed over him. They still had nothing to tie Belinsky to Allenton. While he felt certain there was a reason their perp had fired at Grayson, they needed something concrete to take to a judge.

Through the living room window, he saw Cassidy pull

up next to the SUV. He watched as Sienna slipped inside. Soon, the two women were out of sight.

His phone rang, and seeing Gabe's number on the screen, he pounced. "Please tell me you have something."

"The name of Belinsky's supervisor is Milton Hardy. Here's his number and the address of the company." Gabe recited the information slowly enough that he could plug the digits into his phone.

"Thanks, I'll probably head over there next." He met Grayson's gaze. "Unfortunately we haven't found anything else."

"I'm waiting for the cell phone records," Gabe said. "I asked the company to put a rush on it. They promised to have it to me in an hour."

That was better than he'd hoped. "Excellent. I know you'll work on cross-referencing the numbers. If you find a link to Allenton, let me know."

"Will do. In the meantime, I'll keep digging into Belinsky, but you should know I've got nothing. If he's a crook, he's been flying under the radar."

"That's interesting." In Zeke's experience, guys didn't just go from working a job to shooting at people over night. And if the financial judgment was five years ago, why was Belinsky working for Allenton now? He didn't like that the pieces still didn't fit together. "There must be a connection between Josh Allenton and Toby Belinsky. We just have to find it."

"Working on it. Later." Gabe ended the call.

He turned to Grayson. "Let's get out of here."

"Where are you going?" Officer Alexander asked suspiciously.

"To interview Belinsky's boss." It wasn't easy, but he added, "Do you guys want to ride along?"

"No need as long as you keep us in the loop," Officer Alexander said.

"I will. Thanks." He gestured for Grayson to follow him out. Grayson still had the evidence bags containing the cell phone and weapon. "We'll swing by the lab first. Then to the delivery company."

The trip didn't take too long, but Zeke was still antsy by the time they were speaking with Milton Hardy. After introducing themselves, Zeke asked, "How well do you know Toby Belinsky?"

"Not very. He's quiet, does his job, doesn't give me any trouble." Hardy shrugged. "Why, what's the problem?"

"He's dead."

Milton Hardy's eyes bulged. "He was murdered?"

"No one said anything about murder," Grayson said, his voice testy. "He fired a weapon at a cop, who returned fire. We think he's responsible for several attacks against a woman."

"Really?" Hardy looked shocked. "Look, I don't know what to tell you. When Hardy asked for a couple of days off because he didn't feel well, I didn't argue. He rarely takes time off. But attacking a woman? Shooting a cop?" Hardy shook his head. "I never would have guessed him to be capable of something like that."

"Is he having financial trouble?" Zeke asked.

"Maybe. He took out a loan at the bank a few weeks ago," Hardy said. "I had to send the bank paperwork about his pay and how many hours he works."

Money could be the motivation, but they needed more. How did Allenton find Belinsky? They must have known each other at some point.

From here, it was up to Gabe Melrose to find the

irrefutable connection they needed to keep Sienna and Bailey safe from Allenton's long reach.

By the time Zeke returned to the safe house, Sienna had worn a path in the carpet moving from the front window to the door and back again. She'd played with Bailey while Taylor was kind enough to make spaghetti and meatballs for dinner.

"Who taught you to cook?" Sienna asked.

"My mother." Taylor offered a half smile. "I often had to help make dinner for my younger siblings."

Zeke stepped through the garage door. Their gazes locked. She stepped closer, as if to welcome him home with a hug and a kiss but stopped herself. The grim expression in his gaze made her heart sink.

"You didn't find a connection?" She wasn't sure how much to say in front of Flynn and Taylor. Bailey was too young to understand.

Her daughter pulled herself up and took several steps toward Zeke, lifting her arms in the universal sign of wanting to be held.

"Not yet." Zeke's expression morphed into a wide smile as he bent and lifted Bailey in his arms. The little girl laughed as he swung her from side to side. "Hey, pretty girl." He pressed a kiss on Bailey's cheek. "You sure know how to brighten the mood."

"Again. Do again." Bailey patted his cheeks. Zeke's gaze softened, then he obliged her by swinging her around again.

She told herself not to be depressed, but technically, the time frame she'd given him was running out. If she had to cancel the show, she probably shouldn't go in and do the interview at the TV station.

Although if she canceled that, would the morning show have another guest to put in her slot? Probably not. This was getting complicated, and she still didn't know what to do.

Stay or go?

Watching Zeke play with Bailey made her want to stay. Made her wish their engagement was real. Made her want . . . no, what was she thinking? She'd pledged to never marry again.

Okay, *never* was a really long time. And it was totally unrealistic for her to think she'd never fall in love.

Love. How was it possible she'd fallen in love with Zeke? Her heart swelled, and she had to look away to keep herself from blurting out the truth.

Time to get a grip on reality.

Their situation of being forced together wasn't real. Her feelings toward Zeke were probably commingled with the fact that he'd saved her life, more than once. Besides, even if she did care for Zeke, this wasn't the time to think about her personal life. She had responsibilities to her manager and the fans who'd purchased tickets to her show.

Not to mention her daughter. Allowing Josh to take Bailey even for five minutes was not happening.

She glanced at her watch. Zeke must have noticed

because he set Bailey back on the floor and moved toward her. "There's still time. Rhy has approved for Gabe to work overtime on this. He has just started going through Belinsky's phone records. We're going to find that connection we need."

She desperately wanted to believe that. But her hopes died a little more with each passing minute.

"Dinner will be ready in ten minutes," Taylor said.

Zeke glanced from Taylor to Flynn. "You went out for groceries?"

"Nah, we had them delivered," Flynn said. "You took my car, remember?"

"That's right." Zeke scrubbed his hands over his face. "I'm sure getting a grocery delivery is fine. It's been a long day."

"Even longer for some of us," Flynn said dryly.

When Cassidy had dropped her off, Flynn had peppered her with questions. She'd filled him and Taylor in on the highlights of the day, glossing over the incident where she'd kicked her manager out of the Pfister Hotel.

Then Flynn had called Gabe to talk through what Flynn could do from here. Which only consisted of checking Belinsky's social media.

"What have you been up to?" Zeke asked as he stepped into the kitchen. "Last I heard you were going through Belinsky's social media."

"Yeah, unfortunately the guy hasn't posted much in the past year." Flynn gestured to the image of Toby up on the screen. "I've made a note of each of his social media friends and have been going through their pages to see if I can connect any of them to Allenton."

"Just before Belinsky died, I tried to get him to tell me

who hired him," Zeke admitted. "He said Al, but that was it. Not the full name of Allenton."

"That's interesting," Flynn agreed. "I was able to rule out the ex-girlfriend as a suspect. I found Analise Waverly now Walden on social media. She's married with two kids and lives in Madison. I doubt she's involved."

Flynn had shown Sienna the pictures, and she'd agreed with his assessment. Besides, it seemed to her that Belinsky must have been the shooter.

"Flynn, do you mind putting the computer in the living room?" Taylor asked. "I'd like to set the table."

"Sure." Flynn closed the laptop and stood. "Food is fuel for the brain, and I suspect I'll be going through this for the rest of the night."

"I'll help," Zeke said.

Flynn nodded and carried the laptop into the other room. Sienna propped Bailey's car seat in the chair so that she was able to sit at the table with them.

Taylor set a large pot of noodles on the table, along with another container filled with spaghetti sauce and plump meatballs. She added another basket of garlic bread, the scent making Sienna's mouth water.

Earlier she hadn't been the least bit hungry, but now that Zeke was back, her appetite returned. She hadn't exactly feared for his life, but the shoot-out in Toby Belinsky's backyard was a stark reminder of the danger Zeke and his teammates faced every day.

How difficult it must be for Zeke and Grayson to end someone's life, even as they're protecting their own and those innocent people around them.

"I'd like to say grace," Sienna said once they were seated. No one complained, so she bowed her head. "Lord Jesus, we thank You for this food we are blessed to eat. We are also thankful for the everlasting life You have given us and ask that You please continue to keep us and the rest of the police officers safe in Your care. Amen."

"Amen," Zeke, Flynn, and Taylor echoed.

"Dig in," Zeke added for levity.

They passed around the spaghetti, meatballs, and garlic bread. Sienna helped Bailey with her food between bites of her own meal. The little girl was covered with spaghetti sauce by the time they were finished.

"She's wearing more than she ate," Zeke said with a smile.

"I'll give her a bath when I'm finished with the dishes," Taylor offered.

"I can take care of the dishes," Zeke said. "Flynn is on a roll with the social media stuff, and you cooked. I don't mind cleaning up."

That was something Josh would never have done, but that was mostly because Josh had become spoiled when his parents had become wealthy. Yet he also believed cooking and cleaning was her job, not his.

A true chauvinist, she thought with a sigh. That should have been her first sign that she'd made a mistake in marrying him.

One of many signs she'd ignored or had been too naïve to recognize.

"I'll help with the dishes," she said, rising to her feet. She loved giving Bailey baths, but it wasn't fair to make Taylor clean up after cooking.

"Fine with me," Taylor said. "You haven't let me do much with Bailey since you've been home."

That was true, and really, she probably didn't need a live-in nanny. She'd hired Taylor because it seemed easier than getting a babysitter for her rehearsals, the TV interview, and the three shows. Now, she wasn't so sure. It might be smarter to do short-term nanny stints, like just over the weekend during her shows.

If she was still performing after all of this.

"I think you should do the interview tomorrow," Zeke said as they stood side by side at the kitchen sink. He'd wanted to wash, so she'd begun to dry. "We learned today that Belinsky had taken out a loan. I know that Gabe will find the connection we need. Besides, I don't think it's fair for you to cancel the morning show at the last minute."

"I plan on doing the interview," she said. "But I'm on the fence about moving forward with the performances."

"If we don't find anything to link Belinsky to your ex, then I agree doing the shows might be too risky," Zeke agreed. "It's hard to imagine, but if we're wrong about Belinsky, the shooter is still out there."

Maybe she was being overly cautious, because why would Toby try to avoid being interviewed by the police and, worse, fire his gun at a cop? He must have been hired by Josh.

"I'm leaning toward doing the Milwaukee shows," she said. "But we can discuss that more tomorrow."

"You're supposed to be at the studio by eight o'clock tomorrow morning, so I think we should leave here by seven fifteen, in case we run into traffic."

"Sounds good." She eyed him as she put the last of the dishes away. "Don't work all night, Zeke. You need to sleep."

"We'll get some rest." He flashed a smile. "I'm hoping Gabe will call with good news before the night is over."

She nodded and hung the damp dish towel on the oven handle to dry. "Wake me up if you get good news."

He hesitated, then nodded. "If that's what you want."

There was so much more that she wanted, but she simply nodded. Leaving Flynn and Zeke to their work, she helped dry off Bailey after her bath, then played with the toddler until it was time for her to go to bed.

An hour later, Sienna checked in on the guys. From the frustrated expressions on their faces, she understood there was no point in asking if they'd found anything. She bade them good night and went to bed.

When she awoke at quarter past six the next morning, her first thought was that Zeke hadn't woken her up. Bailey was still sleeping, so she took a quick shower, blow-dried her long, dark hair, then headed to the kitchen for some badly needed coffee.

"Good morning," Zeke greeted her with a faint smile. He gestured to the half-full pot. "It will be ready soon."

"Nothing from Gabe?" she asked, even though she knew the answer.

"Not yet. He quit working about nine o'clock last night. His vision was blurring from staring at the computer screen. He'll start up again at eight this morning. Maybe we'll have good news once the interview is over."

"I'm sure he will." She wasn't convinced, but there was no point in dwelling on the negative now. The upcoming interview was front and center in her mind. She wasn't afraid to sing her praises to the Lord in front of large groups of people—that was simple, heartwarming, and freeing. The exact opposite of what she was about to do. Sitting in front of a live camera to be interviewed by the two Milwaukee Morning show hosts was a bit nerve-racking.

Zeke filled two mugs with coffee. When Bailey woke up, she took some time to care for her daughter. Taylor was in the kitchen making breakfast, but a quick glance at her watch proved they didn't have time to stay.

"We'll grab something on the way," Zeke said.

"Okay." She wasn't sure she could eat much anyway. She gave Bailey a kiss, then followed Zeke to the SUV in the garage. The traffic wasn't terrible, so they made it to the studio in plenty of time.

Zeke had gone through a drive-through fast-food place for breakfast sandwiches. She only took a few bites of hers before setting it aside. Silly to be nervous.

The next hour passed in a flurry of activity. Hair, makeup that seemed way too heavy-handed, and a few tweaks of her sweater and skirt ensemble. Before she knew it, Sienna was standing off camera, waiting for her cue.

"Please join us in welcoming Sienna!" Tiffany, the blond-haired morning show hostess gushed. The small studio audience clapped as Sienna moved to the sofa on the raised platform.

"Thank you for having me," Sienna said with a warm smile.

"Tell us about your recent engagement," Barbie, the dark-haired hostess said. "So exciting to know you got engaged here in your hometown."

While the engagement wasn't real, Sienna found herself relaxing. It was far easier to discuss how wonderful Zeke was than to talk about herself.

When they stopped recording for the first commercial break, Sienna was pleased with how things were going. Tiffany and Barbie were sweet and relaxed. The second part of her interview was focused on her show and her career. To her surprise, the interview ended in what seemed like record time.

"Thanks again," Tiffany said, leading her off the platform. "Maria will take you back to the dressing room."

"Thanks for having me." She followed Maria to the

small dressing room, grateful for the chance to remove the clown makeup. They'd used far more than she did even on show nights.

When that was finished, she grabbed her purse and headed for the door. She was wondering what Dirk had thought of the interview when she stopped abruptly at seeing a familiar face.

"Alice, what are you doing here?" Josh's mother was the last person she'd expected to see here. Obviously, the woman had come to talk to her about giving Josh a second chance.

So not happening.

"Sienna." Alice Allenton always seemed to speak her name in a sneer. It was no secret Alice thought her son could do better.

"How did you get in here?" Sienna asked in confusion.

"You should know money talks," the older woman said with a careless shrug. "I donated some advertising funds in exchange for being allowed to watch the show. I believe my money paid for that big billboard featuring your picture."

The idea of Alice sitting in the audience watching as she gushed about her engagement to Zeke made her feel sick. But then Alice grabbed her arm and shoved something hard against her side. It took Sienna a moment to realize the woman had a gun. "I think it's time we had a little talk, don't you?"

For a moment, she couldn't move as her mind grappled with what was happening. Then she knew. Josh hadn't been the one to hire someone to send notes, then attack her. It had never made sense to her that Josh would suddenly care about his daughter when he hadn't been the least bit happy to learn of her pregnancy.

No, Josh didn't want custody of her daughter.

Alice did.

***

ZEKE LOOKED at his watch for the fifth time in five minutes. What was taking Sienna so long? Maybe she was taking the time to bask in her success. It was well deserved. Her interview had been incredible. Despite her nervousness on the way here, she'd looked completely at ease during the entire conversation. Even while describing how Zeke had proposed at their favorite Italian restaurant, Mario's.

The entire audience had sighed at the romantic gesture. He'd felt like an idiot for not realizing this subject would come up. They should have discussed it, but as it turned out, Sienna handled the questions without hesitation. To the point he felt guilty over the lie they were perpetrating. He could imagine Rhy, Joe, and the other members of the team watching this interview.

In truth, he and Sienna had gone to Mario's for dinner the night of Luke's funeral. Despite their grief, they had gotten caught up on their personal and professional lives.

And he remembered how beautiful she looked as she described her foray into Christian music. How she'd found God and believed in Jesus Christ who'd died for their sins. How blessed she was to have been given a beautiful daughter and the talent to sing music that resonated in her heart.

He'd been so touched and humbled, he'd almost told her how much he'd admired her while they were growing up. How much he'd wanted to ask her out, even if that meant suffering Luke's wrath.

But she had been going through a divorce, not to

mention becoming a single mother of a baby girl, so he'd kept his feelings to himself.

A familiar face walked past, and he instinctively grasped the woman's arm. What was her name? Marta? Martha? Maria?

"Um, excuse me, Maria?" *Yeah, Maria.* "I'm waiting for Sienna. Will you find her for me?"

"Sienna? I think she just left with that older silver-haired woman." Maria waved to the door leading out of the studio. "If you hurry, I'm sure you can catch up to them."

Older silver-haired woman? That didn't make any sense. Without answering, he quickly hurried toward the door. Bursting through, he scanned the area.

And saw them. A silver-haired woman holding Sienna close to her side, walking quickly toward a waiting long, black stretch limo.

Limo? A horrible realization washed over him.

Was that silver-haired woman Josh's mother?

Alice and Tom Allenton. The names of Josh's parents flashed in his mind. Had Belinsky tried to identify Alice as the person who'd hired him?

He broke into a run, kicking himself for leaving his weapon in the glove box of the car. The security at the studio had lured him into a false sense of security. That and there were No Weapons Allowed signs everywhere. "Stop! Police!"

As if they were conjoined at the hip, the two women turned as one to face him. It was then he realized Alice was holding a gun pressed firmly into Sienna's side.

"Don't come any closer," the woman ordered in a raspy voice. "This has nothing to do with you. We're just going to have a little talk, right, Sienna?"

Sienna didn't answer, her gaze clinging to his. He

understood she didn't want to go anywhere with Alice. But the gun pressed into her side didn't leave her much of a choice. A wave of fury hit hard, but he managed to battle it back.

He wasn't the hostage negotiator for the team, but he'd learned a few tricks along the way.

"I'll go with you," he said, slowing to a walk. He didn't want to spook the woman into pulling the trigger. "I'm sure we can work something out that will make everyone happy."

"Stop right there!" Alice repeated harshly. "Or I'll shoot her now and be done with it."

He hoped that was an empty threat, but he was concerned that Alice had the money and power to cover her tracks. After all, she'd gotten this far.

There was no way on earth Rhy would ever believe this woman over him. The Milwaukee DA's office wouldn't either. Rhy's brother-in-law Bax Scala worked as an ADA as did Rhy's cousin Maddy Sinclair.

"You won't get away with this," he said to buy time. "Our tech expert Gabe Melrose has identified the disposable phone you used to communicate with Toby Belinsky." It was a lie, but the flash of concern in her eyes gave him a sense of satisfaction. "Belinsky is dead, but I'm sure you already knew that. It's why you're here now, right? You ran out of bad guys to do your dirty work." He hesitated, hoping she'd comply, but she didn't move. "Walk away and drop the custody battle and we can pretend this never happened."

That was another lie. Two men were dead, and someone had to be held accountable. But he'd say anything to convince Alice to drop the gun and let Sienna go.

"Stop! I'm not kidding. I will shoot," Alice repeated in a cold, emotionally detached tone. "It's easier for us anyway.

With Sienna out of the picture, Josh will get custody of their daughter. And he'll in turn hand the little girl over to me."

"Actually, that's not true," Sienna said quickly. "Josh won't get custody of Bailey. After Zeke and I got engaged, I updated my will to name Zeke as Bailey's guardian if anything happened to me. And you can rest assured, Zeke will never let your son anywhere near my daughter."

The woman recoiled from that information as if she'd been tased. Then she abruptly pulled the gun from Sienna's side and turned the muzzle toward him.

"No!" Sienna threw herself at the older woman, trying to knock her off balance as she reached for the gun at the same time Alice pulled the trigger.

Searing pain caught him off guard, but he didn't hesitate to charge toward them. Sienna had managed to push Alice up against the side of the limo, and the two women struggled for control over the gun.

He reached between them, grabbed the weapon, and wrenched it free. He wanted to toss it far away from where they were standing, but then he remembered the limo driver. There was no sign of the guy. Had he taken off during the scuffle? Or was he still inside the vehicle? Either way, he couldn't risk the driver being loyal enough to Alice to go for the gun. Rather than tossing it aside, he slipped her gun into the hollow of his back.

At some level, he heard the screams and shouts of people running away due to the gunfire. Was there a cop nearby? He hoped so. He also hoped someone had called 911. He could use some backup, especially to get Alice secured.

No easy feat since he didn't even have his handcuffs on him.

As if reading his mind, Sienna said, "Here, use this." She removed her purse from her shoulder. In two quick movements, she released the strap from either end of the bag. Then she handed him the long thin cord.

Perfect. He smiled his gratitude, then turned his attention to the woman who'd started this nightmare.

And who had nearly succeeded in kidnapping Sienna.

"Alice Allenton, you're under arrest for threatening to kill Sienna and for the potential murder of a police officer." After nudging Sienna out of the way, he used his full weight to press Alice's slight frame against the side of the limo. The smaller frail woman was no match for his strength and bulk.

As he spoke, he looped one end of the purse strap around her wrists, then brought the other end of the strap between her wrists so he could tie them together. Ignoring her whimper, he continued, "You have the right to remain silent. Anything you say can and will be used against you in a court of law. You have the right to an attorney." He paused, frowning as the next part of the Miranda warning failed to materialize in his mind.

A wave of dizziness hit hard. He tried to fight it off until he saw the blood running down his arm. The pain in his shoulder was getting worse to the point he couldn't feel his fingers in his left hand.

Dazed, he realized he'd been shot.

CHAPTER FIFTEEN

Seeing the blood running down Zeke's arm spurred Sienna into action. She yanked on the limo car door and poked her head inside. The driver sat frozen behind the wheel. "Did you call 911?" she asked. When he shook his head, she sighed. "Get out of the car."

"I—I'm not involved in this," he sputtered, pushing his driver's side door open.

"You didn't step up to stop it either," she said harshly. "And what would you have done if Alice pushed me into the car at gunpoint? Would you have driven away?"

"I don't know anything about a gun!" The driver looked panicked now. As he should. She didn't have time to get into the details surrounding Alice's hiring him now. Zeke needed medical attention. And based on the way he was slumped against the side of the limo, he needed it fast!

"Give me your jacket." She gestured for the black coat the driver wore. When he didn't strip off the garment fast enough, she started to yank it off him.

"Okay, okay." He shrugged out of the coat.

She quickly wrapped it around Zeke's shoulders. Then

she noticed Alice was moving away. "Oh no you don't." She grabbed the older woman by the back of her expensive blouse and yanked her back. "You shot a cop. You're not going anywhere."

As blood continued to run freely down Zeke's arm, she glanced at the driver. "If you don't want to be arrested as an accomplice, hold on to this woman for me." She thrust Alice toward him. "Don't let her go, understand?"

"Yeah, sure." The driver did as she asked, grabbing Alice by the shoulders but holding her at arm's length as if she might bite. And who knows? Maybe Alice would.

Satisfied her ex-mother-in-law wasn't going to escape, she turned her attention back to Zeke. "Sit down." She gently pushed him to the ground. "I need to look at your injury."

"Call for help," Zeke said in a raspy voice.

Before she could respond, she heard the wail of sirens. She had hoped someone had called in the shooting. "Help is on the way. Let me see your injury."

"Left shoulder," he said, leaning his head back against the side of the limo and closing his eyes.

Swallowing hard, she leaned in to examine the oozing wound located in the hollow of his shoulder. She was no nurse and only had normal first-aid experience born of being a mother, but it looked bad.

Very bad.

Remembering how Zeke had tried—and failed—to save Belinsky made her strip off her sweater, pressing it against his wound. Then she reached around him to feel along his back.

Her fingers found more blood. The bullet had gone all the way through!

Both the entry and exit wounds needed to be cared for.

She pushed him against the frame of the limo with all her might, silently praying the ambulance and police officers would arrive soon.

Please, Lord Jesus, help me save Zeke's life!

The sirens grew louder. She continued to pray as the squads came to a stop and officers emerged from the cars.

"This is MPD Officer Zeke Hawthorne," she said. "He's been shot by that woman over there. Her name is Alice Allenton."

Thankfully, the officers didn't quibble. One dropped to his knees beside her, while two others grabbed Alice from the limo driver.

Zeke groaned as the officer examined the wound.

"We need an ambulance," Sienna said.

"That's them now," the officer said, nodding to the ambulance that pulled up alongside the squads. She was thankful to see two paramedics emerge from the vehicle. One had reddish hair but had similar facial features to Rhy.

When he came closer, she saw his name tag read Finnegan. So he was one of the siblings. She moved aside when the two paramedics brought their medical bag and gurney over.

"This is Zeke Hawthorne; he works for Rhy," she said.

"Got it," the red-haired guy said. "Hey, Zeke, it's Colin. We're going to get you to Trinity Medical Center, okay?"

Zeke opened his eyes, appearing confused for a moment. Then he nodded. "Make sure they arrest Alice Allenton," he said.

"I've got her," another officer said.

"Her gun." Zeke struggled to sit up, but Colin and the other paramedic pushed him back down. "I have the gun she used to shoot me. In my back waistband."

The officer reached behind him and pulled out the weapon. "We have it."

"Good." Zeke closed his eyes, and this time, his head slumped to the side. It was as if he'd used up every last bit of his strength to tie up the loose ends.

"Colin? Is he going to make it?" she asked.

"We're going to do to everything possible," Colin Finnegan assured her. "But I need you to move out of the way."

She nodded, rose on shaky legs, and moved away to give them room. The two paramedics worked as an amazing team as they connected equipment to Zeke's chest, started an IV, and dressed both wounds.

Moments later, they had Zeke on their gurney and were wheeling him to the waiting ambulance. She took a step toward them, intending to ask if she could ride along, when the officer who'd first responded to the scene caught her arm.

"Ma'am? I'm going to need your statement," he said, his expression apologetic. "Don't worry, Hawthorne is in good hands."

Zeke was in God's hands, but she still didn't want him to be taken away without her. "Can't you follow me to the hospital?"

"Sienna? What's going on?" To her shock, Rhy Finnegan came striding toward her. "Where's Zeke?"

"In the ambulance with Colin." She gripped his arm. "I need to go to the hospital."

Rhy nodded, then glanced at the officer. "You can take her statement but make it quick. When she's finished, I'll take her to Trinity Medical Center. If you have follow-up questions, you can contact me."

"Sure thing, Captain Finnegan," the officer said respectfully.

Knowing Rhy was there helped keep her calm. He remained at her side while she explained how her former mother-in-law, Alice Allenton, had surprised her inside the TV studio. And that she'd forced her to leave at gunpoint. When she described how she'd lied to Alice about making Zeke her daughter's guardian, tears filled her eyes.

"It's my fault she shot him," Sienna whispered. "If I hadn't made up that story about Zeke being Bailey's legal guardian, she wouldn't have tried to kill him."

"Sounds like she would have killed you, Sienna," Rhy said gently. "I know Zeke is glad things went this way instead."

"I'm not." She swiped at her eyes, anger flashing through her. "I should have suspected something the moment I saw her standing in the studio! I should have turned and run to find Zeke instead of going along with her."

"Hey, don't do that," Rhy chided. "There's no point in rehashing what you could have done. Knowing Zeke, he'll shoulder the blame, thinking there was something he should have done differently too. All we can do is move forward from here."

"This is all related to custody of your daughter?" the officer asked in confusion. "The woman with her wrists bound, Alice Allenton, shot a cop because she wanted full custody of your daughter?"

"Yes." Hearing him say it so bluntly was horrifying. How anyone would take such drastic action to force a mother into giving up her only child was incomprehensible. She took a deep breath and continued with her statement. "She admitted to me that if my ex-husband was able to obtain custody, he would turn around and give my daughter to her. I had no idea she was the reason behind his sudden desire for custody. When I said Zeke would be named as Bailey's guardian, she abruptly pointed the gun at him. I tried to grab the weapon from her, but she pulled the trigger. Zeke charged forward to help. We used the strap of my purse to tie her wrists. Then I told the limo driver to hold on to her until you arrived."

The officer looked at her in admiration. "Smart thinking Ms. Reynolds. We'll talk to the limo driver too. Other than that, I think I have enough for now."

"I'd like Alice Allenton charged for kidnapping and threatening Sienna with a deadly weapon and the attempted murder of a police officer," Rhy said. "Now if you don't mind, I'd like to take Sienna to the hospital."

"Of course, Captain." The officer stepped back. "We'll continue to process the scene. If I learn anything new, I'll let you know."

"Thanks." Rhy took her arm, steering her away from the limo. "Let's get out of here."

She was more than ready to leave the scene. Glancing down at hands that were stained with Zeke's blood, she prayed with every ounce of faith and hope in her body.

Please, Lord Jesus, spare Zeke's life.

ZEKE AWOKE to a throbbing pain that reverberated through his entire body. At first he didn't understand, then slowly the events outside the TV studio formed in his mind.

Alice Allenton had shot him.

Now that he was more aware of his surroundings, he could pinpoint the source of the pain as his left shoulder.

He lifted his right hand up and tried to touch the injury, but he must have jerked some wires because alarms began to beep loudly.

"Zeke?" Sienna's concerned features swam into his line of sight. "You're awake?"

"Kinda." He looked around what was clearly a hospital room. "What happened? Is Alice in custody?"

"She is, yes. And you had surgery on your shoulder." Sienna rested her hand on his arm as a nurse entered the room.

"Mr. Hawthorne, I'm Emily, your nurse for the evening." Emily looked as if she might have graduated from high school yesterday, not college. "Would you like some ice chips?"

"Please." His voice was hoarse, his mouth drier than the desert.

He would have taken the whole cup, but she didn't give him that option. Setting the cup of ice chips aside, she smiled again. "I'm going to check your vital signs."

Obviously, he didn't have a choice. When the young Emily finished, she asked if he wanted something for pain.

"Not yet. Maybe in an hour," he said. "I need to understand a few things first." The pain was bad, but he couldn't exist in a drug-induced fog either.

"Okay, I'll be back in an hour," Emily said cheerfully.

He scowled. Easy for her to be all smiley. She wasn't hooked up to a bunch of monitors fantasizing about a cup of ice chips.

"Emily has been taking good care of you," Sienna said, sensing his ire. She took his right hand in hers. "And the surgeon is very optimistic that you'll regain full use of your left arm."

The thought of not fully recovering hadn't occurred to

him. Swallowing against a surge of panic, he tried to nod. If the doctor was hopeful, then he would be too. Besides, a good attitude was half the battle. Or so he hoped. "Okay. What happened with Alice? Did she lawyer up? Did Gabe find anything connecting her to Toby Belinsky and Ken Holt?"

"I'm not sure," Sienna said. "I haven't left the hospital."

That stunned him. "You need to head back to the safe house to be with your daughter."

"Flynn brought Taylor and Bailey here for a few hours." Her smile faded. "Flynn kept me company as we waited to hear about your surgery."

He felt guilty for putting her through this. And for the first time since he'd awoken, he realized it was over. The danger, their fake engagement, her need to stay at the safe house.

Over.

A knock at the door interrupted his thoughts. He turned his head to see Rhy entering the room. The look of satisfaction etched in his boss's features made him sigh in relief. "You have the evidence we need to indict Alice."

"We do," Rhy agreed. "It helped that we found Alice's burner phone. Gabe tracked that number to calls made to both Toby Belinsky and Ken Holt." Rhy's expression sobered. "The gun Belinsky used to shoot at Grayson matches the bullet taken from Ken Holt's body. We believe Belinsky was told to kill Holt and to leave his body at the rental property."

Zeke wasn't surprised. As much as Alice hadn't hesitated to fire at him, he didn't see her shooting Holt and putting him in the White Gull Bay rental home. "How did Alice find Belinsky?"

"Gabe finally found that connection; turns out that

Belinsky's mother, Louise, once worked for Alice and Tom. They offered him a significant amount of money to take care of Sienna."

He nodded slowly. "What about Sienna's ex-husband? Is he involved?"

Rhy shrugged. "That is still an unknown. We asked the LAPD to pick him up and keep him for questioning as we spoke with his mother. So far, Josh is doing all the talking, while the old lady is keeping her mouth shut."

He shifted on the bed, then grimaced when a flash of pain hit hard. Wow, who knew surgery hurt so much? "Figures Allenton threw his own mother under the bus," Zeke said through gritted teeth.

"True that," Rhy agreed. "Josh said he went along with the custody request because his mom was footing the legal fees. He claims he harbors no ill feelings toward Sienna." Rhy shrugged, then added, "I will say Josh Allenton dropped the custody request faster than a hot potato once he knew we had his mommy in custody. And that she wasn't getting out anytime soon."

That made Zeke smile. "Yeah, but Mommy has money. I'm sure she'll get out on bail."

"Not necessarily," Rhy said. "Attempted murder of a police officer is a hefty charge. As is kidnapping with a deadly weapon. I've spoken to my brother-in-law, Bax Scala, who is the ADA on the case. He plans to portray Mommy as a serious flight risk so that she won't get out on bail."

"I hope he's successful." All too often criminals he and other cops worked hard to toss behind bars ended up back on the streets.

But he trusted Bax Scala to do his best. Rhy and the rest of the tactical team would make sure to tie up all the loose ends in the case.

From here, justice would be at the hands of the legal system. All he could do was pray that Alice would be found guilty of her crimes.

"I guess I won't be back to work for a few days," he finally said.

Rhy barked out a laugh. "Try a couple of months. But don't worry, your spot on the team is secure. Just make sure you follow doctor's orders, understand?"

"Yeah. I understand." He shifted again, then added, "Thanks, Rhy."

"I'll check in on you tomorrow." Rhy turned away.

There was a long silence in the wake of Rhy's absence. He glanced at Sienna. "You're still going to perform this weekend?"

"Yes." She smiled. "I feel like that's what God wants me to do."

"Good." He tried to return her smile but was keenly aware that when the weekend was over, Sienna and Bailey would move on to the next show. Chicago, if he remembered correctly.

And then Louisville.

Then . . . he couldn't remember. It didn't really matter. He would miss her and Bailey like crazy. But he wouldn't stand in her way either. She'd been through a lot and deserved to have the life she'd always dreamed of.

"I'll be fine here," he said. "I'm sure Rhy won't mind if you use the safe house for a few more days. You need to rest up for three days of back-to-back concerts."

"I almost lost you," Sienna said in a low voice. "I never should have lied about granting you custody of Bailey. I should have known she'd try to eliminate you as a threat."

"Hey, I thought that was brilliant," he quickly protested. "Seriously, it was smart of you to throw a wrench in her plan. That information knocked her off balance. And I'm glad things worked out the way they did. It was worth getting shot to have her in custody."

"I've been praying nonstop since you were injured, wishing there was more that I could do to make up for what happened," she murmured. "I'm thankful God answered my prayers."

"Hey, I'm fine." The sheen of tears in her eyes hit him like a sledgehammer. "This isn't your fault. I'm the idiot who left his weapon in the glove box of the vehicle. I shouldn't have assumed the security of the TV studio was enough to cover you."

A tremulous smile tugged at her lips. "Rhy said you would blame yourself."

"The only person responsible for this is Alice herself. Not you. Not me." He managed a more convincing smile. "God put us exactly where we needed to be to keep your daughter safe."

"You're right." She nodded, then surprised him by bending over to kiss him. "I love you, Zeke."

"I—uh." He wasn't sure what to say. She probably loved him like a brother. "I love you too," he said. "And I wish I could be there to see your show. I'm sure you'll bring the house down."

She tipped her head to the side, regarding him thoughtfully. "I love you, and I was hoping I could convince you to travel with me while you're recovering. If you're not interested in traveling, then I'll cancel the rest of my concerts and stay here in Milwaukee."

"Wait, what are you talking about?" Had he missed something? Maybe the drugs had fried a few brain cells because he wasn't following. "There's no reason to cancel your tour now that we have Alice behind bars. Even if she gets out on bail, we'll arrange for a no contact order to keep her from coming anywhere near you and Bailey."

"I know I don't have to cancel my tour, but I don't want to leave you." Now her expression was exasperated. "I love you, Zeke. I loved being engaged to you, and I want to see where our love might take us."

"Love me? Are you sure?" He searched her gaze.

"Yes, I love you. And I want to spend more time with you. Time doing things other than dodging gunmen." Her tone was light, but the expression in her blue eyes was intense. "I know you've always viewed me as a younger sister, but things have changed. I guess I'm hoping the attraction I feel for you isn't one sided."

A sense of relief washed over him. "It's not," he admitted. "I love you too." He tugged on her hand. "Kiss me again."

She laughed and obliged.

He didn't want to let her go, but his young nurse poked her head into the room. "How are you feeling?"

"Great." Well, his heart was great. His shoulder, not so much. "But I wouldn't mind taking that pain pill now."

"I'll be right back," Emily promised.

"I guess I should go," Sienna said. "I feel guilty leaving Bailey with Taylor and Flynn for so long. I'll check back with you tomorrow morning, okay?"

"That's fine." He didn't blame her for wanting to be reunited with her daughter. "Don't worry about me, knock them dead tomorrow night. Saturday and Sunday too."

She smiled and kissed him again. Then she waited until the pain medicine lulled him to sleep before slipping away.

Despite basking in the glow of Sienna's love, it was a long night. The nurses woke him up to take his vitals every few hours, and the pain in his shoulder was fierce. But by the morning, he was anxious to speak to the surgeon and to find a way to bust out of there.

Turns out, hospitals were not a good place to rest and recover.

The surgeon came by early and reiterated what Sienna had heard. He was confident that Zeke would regain full range of motion in his left arm as long as he followed through with his physical therapy and home exercises.

Then he agreed to let Zeke go home later that afternoon.

Sienna visited as promised but couldn't linger too long as she and Bailey and Taylor were moving from the safe house to a hotel. "Not the Pfister," she added with a smile, but they had a set of adjoining room at the American Lodge.

When Rhy showed up at nearly five o'clock in the afternoon, he was more than ready to go. But to his surprise, rather than taking him home, Rhy drove him to the homestead, the six-bedroom home in Brookland where Rhy and his eight siblings had grown up.

"You can't be alone," Rhy had said with a shrug. "Devon is happy to help. And we have a small outing planned tonight anyway."

"I'm not sure I'm up for that," he admitted.

"You will be. Trust me," Rhy said.

After a short nap and a meal of toast and soup, he was surprised when Rhy insisted he dress in dress slacks and a polo shirt that was stretched over his sling. He felt like an idiot when Colin Finnegan and his wife, emergency department Dr. Faye Finnegan, came to pick him up from the homestead.

Then he understood. "We're heading to the Sinatra Music Center?"

"Yep. Sienna wanted you to come to the show if you

were able," Colin said. "And we're here to provide any medical care you might need."

He was touched by Sienna's thoughtfulness, although he was not happy to see someone coming toward the car with a wheelchair. "I can walk," he said gruffly.

"Don't argue. It's going to be the best seat in the house," Colin said.

His boss's brother wasn't lying. The music center usher pushed him up to the front of the stage, locked the wheels into place, then found two seats for Colin and Faye nearby.

Glancing behind him, he was in awe of the packed house. Amazing that this many people had come out to see Sienna.

At exactly eight o'clock, the curtain rose, and the music swelled. Sienna stepped out on stage, looked directly at him, then took the microphone in her hand. She was dressed in a modest gown, her hair down.

"This song is dedicated to the man I love, Zeke Hawthorne, who selflessly risked his life for mine." She smiled at him. "I was given permission by the creators to perform one of my favorite songs called *The Blessing*. Because Zeke is a blessing to me."

He felt his jaw drop with surprise, wondering if Rhy, Colin, and Faye had known she'd planned to kick off her tour this way.

When she began to sing, a hush fell over the crowd. The woman he loved sang her praise to the Lord, softly and poignantly at first, then with more feeling. As the crescendo grew, people surged from their seats, lifting their arms overhead and swaying along with the song. Many even sang along regardless of their ability to carry a tune.

Never in his life had he felt closer to God than in that moment.

And when the final notes drifted away, he wished he could join in the thundering applause.

Sienna was something special. And he knew he must have done something right in his life to have been blessed with her love.

EPILOGUE

Two weeks later . . .

Sienna hugged Taylor. "Thanks for everything you did for me and Bailey."

"You're welcome." Taylor hugged her back, then gave Bailey a big hug and kiss before leaving.

Taylor had decided she didn't want to continue traveling with Sienna and Bailey. And Zeke. Really, Sienna couldn't blame her. Taylor's services weren't needed. Zeke was becoming an expert at caring for Bailey. He didn't have full use of his left arm and shoulder, but he'd managed to master the art of changing her daughter's diapers with minimal use of his left hand.

They'd taken the train from Chicago and Milwaukee several times so Zeke could keep his physical therapy appointments. They were staying at Zeke's house in Greenland between shows. Since most of her performances were three nights over the weekend, he'd insisted on tagging along since he was off work anyway due to his injury.

Sienna had loved having Zeke spend time with her and Bailey. The response to her shows had been incredible, but she had already planned to finish this tour at Christmas, without renewing for next year. At least, not right away. As much as she loved performing the Lord's music, she wasn't interested in traveling from one city to the next for the foreseeable future. Bailey deserved more stability than that.

Besides, Zeke would have to return to work, likely by the first of the year. Her tentative plan at this point was to finish her tour, then settle in Milwaukee permanently.

Although she and Zeke hadn't really discussed their future. Between her shows and his recovery, they'd been taking things day by day.

"Taylor will find another nanny placement," Zeke said, misreading her silence. "I think she was bored here."

"Oh, I agree. She will." She turned to Zeke. "How was physical therapy?"

"Great. Supposedly I'm making good progress, although I still have a long way to go."

"Don't rush it," she warned.

"Who me?" he asked in mock innocence. She knew him well enough to read the frustration at not being able to do certain things. "I hope you don't mind, but I made reservations at Mario's for dinner tonight." He glanced at his watch. "We'll have to hit the road soon. Rhy and Devon agreed to watch Bailey."

She wanted to protest, but Bailey enjoyed spending time with Rhy and Devon's daughter, Colleen. "I should have asked Taylor to stay one night."

"Nah, this will work out fine," Zeke said. "Trust me."

She did trust Zeke, and Rhy too. She would have been happy to stay home, but Zeke looked so happy at going out for dinner, she didn't want to burst his bubble.

"Sure thing. Let me pack some of Bailey's things together."

Ninety minutes later, she and Zeke were sitting in a quiet table at Mario's. The light shimmered from the diamond on her left hand. When she glanced up at Zeke, he smiled. "I wanted to come here tonight for a specific reason," he said, once they'd placed their order.

"Did you get an update on the case from Rhy?" She assumed they'd spoken earlier, and that was when Zeke had asked Rhy to babysit. She braced herself for bad news. "Is Alice still in jail?"

"Yes, she's in jail and not going anywhere," Zeke assured her. He reached over to take her left hand in his. "Do you remember the Milwaukee Morning show interview? When you said I'd proposed at Mario's, our favorite restaurant?"

She flushed, remembering all too well. "I shouldn't have said that," she began.

"Sienna. Will you please marry me? For real?"

She caught her breath. "Are you sure? Bailey and I are a package deal, and I would understand if that was a bit much . . ."

"I love you. I love Bailey," Zeke interrupted. "And I very much want to marry you." He stood, then went down on one knee. "If you want something other than my mother's engagement ring, we'll head to the jewelry store on the way home. You can pick out something better."

"No, I don't want anything else." The thought of wearing his mother's ring was heartwarming. "I only want you, Zeke."

He smiled. "Is that a yes?"

"Yes. Yes, I'd love to marry you." She stood when he did, and they hugged. Awkwardly because he couldn't use his left arm, but it was a sweet embrace all the same. He kissed her, sealing the deal.

"Ah, Sienna," he murmured as they resumed their seats. "You'll have to let me know your plans. I have a feeling the minute I put my house up for sale I'll be inundated with offers, so we need to have an idea of where we're going to live."

"Sell? I don't want you to sell." She lightly touched his arm. "I'm committed to this tour, but when it's over, I'd like to settle down here in town. With you."

"Really?" He looked shocked. "Are you sure? Your performances get better and better each time. The spiritual energy you bring to the room is palpable. After your last show in Chicago, I thought the fans would refuse to leave. I can't believe you wouldn't want to keep going. To keep sharing your talent with the world."

"I can do that in other ways. I would never ask you to give up your job for mine. And I like the idea of Bailey growing up here like we did." She smiled. "I love you, Zeke. The tour is nice, but that's not the only way we can honor God."

"Like the song you dedicated to me, 'The Blessing,'" he said. "For our children and their children and their children."

"Yes, exactly like that." She nodded. "Together, we can do anything."

"Amen," Zeke whispered. Then he stood and drew her in for another kiss.

Despite her past with Josh, she knew she was making the right decision to marry Zeke. He was a true blessing from God.

In a way Josh or his mother would never understand.

•   •   •

I HOPE you enjoyed Zeke and Sienna's story. If you want to hear a beautiful Christian song, look up "The Blessing" on YouTube. The beautiful lyrics will warm your heart and bring tears to your eyes.

Are you ready to read Flynn and Taylor's story? Click here!

DEAR READER

Thanks so much for reading my Oath of Honor series. I'm truly blessed to have wonderful readers like you. I hope you enjoyed Zeke and Sienna's story. I've been having so much fun bringing the Finnegans and even the Callahans back into these books. *Flynn* will be available soon, followed by *Cassidy*. I hope you decide to finish the series with me!

Don't forget, you can purchase eBooks or audiobooks directly from my website will receive a 15% discount by using the code **LauraScott15**.

I adore hearing from my readers! I can be found through my website at https://www.laurascottbooks.com, via Facebook at https://www.facebook.com/LauraScott Books, Instagram at https://www.instagram.com/laurascott books/, and Twitter https://twitter.com/laurascottbooks. Please take a moment to subscribe to my YouTube channel at youtube.com/@LauraScottBooks-wr1xl?sub_confirmation=1. Also, take a moment to sign up for my monthly newsletter to learn about my new book releases! All subscribers receive a free novella not available for purchase on any platform.

Until next time,
Laura Scott
PS: Read on for a sneak peek of *Flynn*.

FLYNN

Chapter One

Glass broke from somewhere downstairs as nanny Taylor Templeton was giving Max a bottle at three in the morning. With a frown she stood, cradling the three-month-old baby close as she moved toward the bedroom door. Then something made her turn and douse the small lamp on the nightstand, plunging the room into darkness.

The Millers were asleep, or so she assumed. Robin and Steve Miller were second cousins on her mom's side of the family. When they'd learned she had experience as a live-in-nanny, they'd hired her to help with Max now that Robin Miller was returning to work. The large two-story house in Brookland, Wisconsin, was very nice, and the Millers were decent people.

She hovered in the open doorway, listening intently. Had she imagined the sound? Maybe Robin or Steve had woken up in the middle of the night and had dropped a glass of water. She could be battling a wave of fear for no reason at all.

Then a creaking sound reached her ears.

Someone was coming up the stairs!

Without giving herself time to think, she darted across the hall from the nursery to her bedroom. She left both doors open, fearing that closing them would catch the attention of whoever was coming up the stairs. Then she grabbed her phone from the nightstand where she'd had it charging.

The thud of a footstep on the landing made her shrink away from the bed. Spotting the walk-in closet, she quietly opened the door and stepped inside. She didn't close the door because it sometimes squeaked. Besides, she had to assume the intruder was looking for money, and if so, he would have no reason to come inside her room.

Or so she hoped.

Pressing herself into the corner of the closet against her clothes, she fought to breathe normally, despite the frantic beat of her heart. Her last live-in nanny assignment had brought a level of danger, so it was possible she was overreacting.

Steve could have dropped the glass, cleaned it up, and was returning to the master suite. Yes, the more she thought about it, the more she realized she was being ridiculous. There was no reason to be afraid.

She stepped toward the partially open closet door.

Pop! Pop! Pop! Pop!

The four shots were somewhat muffled but loud enough to reach her. Every muscle in her body froze at the implication.

Gunfire? Had the intruder shot and killed the Millers?

Taylor opened her mouth to scream but managed to swallow the sound without uttering a word. She needed to call 911, but her fingers didn't want to cooperate. Max continued to suckle his bottle, thankfully oblivious to the danger.

Then she saw a man dressed in black moving past the open doorway of her room. She caught a brief glimpse of his face, especially his prominent nose and bearded face. Her heart nearly burst out of her chest as she recoiled from the closet door. She lowered herself to the floor, scooting into the corner and bending over to make herself as small as possible.

She didn't dare call 911, fearing the sound of her voice would lead the gunman to her hiding spot. Instead, she opened her text message app and scrolled through to the last message she had exchanged with Flynn Ryerson, a Milwaukee cop she'd met on her last assignment. She always kept her phone on silent, so she didn't hesitate to send a text, despite knowing he wouldn't likely see it at this hour of the morning.

A gunman is in the house!

She held the phone screen against the bottom of the blanket wrapped around the baby to minimize the glow of light. The seconds ticked by with excruciating slowness. Then she saw the flash as Flynn responded.

Get out!

I can't. He's in the hallway. I'm hiding in the closet with the baby.

Where?

Taylor texted him the address. The minute she hit send, a muffled thud sent her pulse skyrocketing. Was the intruder looking for the baby?

For her?

Lord Jesus, keep us safe in Your care!

Knowing Flynn was on the way, Taylor tried to remain calm. Maybe the gunman wouldn't stick around. She belatedly realized Max had stopped taking the bottle. She needed to burp him but was afraid to move. He squirmed in her arms as if he were uncomfortable. What if he started to cry?

Bitter fear coated her tongue. With exaggerated slowness, she placed her phone screen down on the floor beside her to free up her hands. Gently shifting the baby in her arms, she settled him upright against her shoulder. She prayed he wouldn't start crying or make any other sound that would give them away.

He didn't.

Rubbing circles over Max's back, she strained to listen. The silence was not reassuring. She half expected the closet door to swing open revealing the gunman.

But then she heard more footsteps. Was the gunman leaving? She was afraid to move, to take another look.

Max burped. She held her breath, hoping and praying the gunman hadn't heard the sound. If he was really heading down the stairs, it wasn't likely.

A flash of light nearly made her scream. A flashlight? Was the intruder still searching for them? Biting her lip hard to keep from crying out, she sat frozen with Max on her shoulder, expecting the beam of light to grow closer.

Then it was gone.

She held her breath until she grew dizzy. By some miracle, Max had fallen asleep against her. She stayed where she was, imagining the intruder going methodically through each room in the house.

A wailing police siren filled her with hope. She felt certain Flynn had called 911 on her behalf, and the local cops were on their way. She forced herself to stand, using the wall for support as her knees felt like overcooked noodles.

Taylor peered through the gap of the half-open closet door. She didn't see anyone, and she couldn't hear anything either.

Except for the sirens that grew louder and louder.

If the intruder was smart, he'd bolt out of there before the cops arrived. Still, she hesitated, fear crippling her. Then she heard a loud crash of a door being forced open. She jumped, startling the baby.

"Taylor! Where are you?"

Flynn's shout was accompanied by the sound of pounding footsteps. She moved toward the doorway of her room, risking a quick glance out the door. She nearly sobbed in relief as Flynn rushed toward her.

"Taylor. Are you okay?" He wrapped his arms around her and Max. "You're not hurt?"

"F-fine." She was shivering, partially from the cold, but more so because of the horrifying experience. "Y-you need to ch-check on Robin and Steve. I—heard gunshots. Four gunshots."

Flynn's expression was grim as he turned to look over his shoulder. She noticed now that two uniformed officers had followed him up the stairs. They took a moment to poke their heads into the nursery, then made their way down the hall, their weapons raised as they approached the closed door of the master suite.

Taylor turned her face into Flynn's shoulder as the officers opened the door and entered the room. It didn't take long for them to return.

"Two victims, male and female, were killed in their bed," an officer with the name tag of Rawson said grimly. "Each victim was shot twice."

"Robin and Steve Miller." She whispered the names of Max's parents. The news was exactly what she'd expected, but hearing the blunt words sent a wave of panic washing over her. Not just because the baby in her arms was now an orphan.

No, the worst part was that she'd gotten a glimpse of the gunman. She was the sole witness to a double homicide.

And from the way this guy had stealthily entered the home and ruthlessly killed Max's parents, she felt certain he wouldn't balk at finding and silencing her too.

***

FLYNN DID NOT like this situation one bit. He glanced at the Brookland PD officers who were regarding Taylor with veiled suspicion.

"This is Taylor Templeton. She's a live-in nanny," he explained. "I know her from a previous case."

The officers exchanged a dubious glance. "That's fine. We'll need her to come down to the station for questioning."

"I know, and she will. But she deserves a chance to change her clothes and get stuff for the baby." Flynn's blood ran cold at the thought of the gunman finding Taylor and the baby hiding in the closet. He wasn't even sure how he'd managed to wake up to her text message, but he was glad he had. He could feel her shaking and knew she was on the verge of a breakdown. Not that he blamed her. "Give us a few minutes, okay?"

"Fine. But don't touch anything outside these two rooms," Officer Rawson warned, gesturing to Taylor's room and the nursery.

When they were alone, he smoothed a hand down Taylor's back to reassure her. "I'm sorry about this, but you need to change and pack a bag. For yourself and the baby."

Taking a long slow breath, she nodded and eased back. "Thank you for coming."

"Of course." He frowned. "Are you sure you're okay?"

"Um, yeah. I think so." She didn't sound at all confident. He eyed her with concern. Taylor was only twenty-four years old, much younger than his thirty-one, but she appeared older now that she'd come face-to-face with death.

"Why don't you let me hold the baby?" He kept his tone soothing. "We can't stay here, Taylor. We need to go."

She seemed to pull herself together. "I know. Here, take him. His name is Max." She gently pressed the baby into his arms. "I don't understand why this is happening," she murmured as she turned to grab an overnight case from the closet. "Why would someone murder the Millers?"

"I don't know." Flynn gazed down at the sleeping baby lying in the crook of his elbow. The poor kid had barely come into this world and was already an orphan. Then he glanced back at her. "But you can rest assured the police won't rest until they find and arrest the man who did this."

She gave a jerky nod. "Will you please turn around so I can change? Don't leave," she quickly added. "Just turn around."

Flynn did as she asked. He wanted to question her about what had transpired but reminded himself this wasn't his case. He was a Milwaukee tactical team police officer out of the seventh district. He and his teammates didn't have jurisdiction in Brookland.

However, the captain of their team, Rhyland Finnegan, happened to live in Brookland and knew many of the local police officers on a first-name basis. Rhy and their team lieutenant, Joe Kingsley—who was married to Elly Finnegan, Rhy's baby sister—had a penchant for getting information from other jurisdictions.

It was a little early to call Joe or Rhy, so Flynn figured he'd wait until after Taylor had given her statement to contact his boss. Maybe by then he'd know more about what had transpired here.

His humble opinion was that this was a professional hit. Striking each victim with two gunshots was overkill, but it also sent a grim message.

And clearly Taylor was in danger now too.

"Okay. I'm ready."

He turned to find Taylor was dressed in a pair of snug blue jeans and a light-blue cable sweater. She had her blond hair pulled into a ponytail, her bright-blue eyes wide and fearful. She had a small suitcase on the floor beside her. He managed a smile. "You're all set?"

"I, uh, need toiletries from the bathroom." She swallowed hard, as if she were nervous about leaving the room. "Then I'll grab some things for Max."

"Let's go." He nudged the bedroom door open with his elbow. "You're safe now," he added.

"Am I?" She shook her head as she brushed past him. She darted in and out of the bathroom, shoving toiletries into her bag, then moved into the nursery. Five minutes later, she emerged with an overstuffed diaper bag.

Her suitcase and the diaper bag were stark reminders that traveling with a woman and a baby wasn't simple or quick. His buddy Zeke Hawthorne had experienced this firsthand a few weeks ago when he'd played the role of fiancé and bodyguard to his best friend's sister. Zeke had taken a bullet to the shoulder and was out on medical leave, or he'd have called him for backup.

Well, maybe not since Zeke and Sienna were engaged to be married for real and were also currently in Louisville for Sienna's next Christian music concert. No, he couldn't call Zeke, but there were seven other officers who would come to his aid if needed.

"We need to grab Max's car seat." Taylor's voice broke into his thoughts as she headed down the stairs to the main floor. Still carrying Max, he followed.

"Ms. Templeton?" Another uniformed officer waited in the kitchen. "Are you ready to go with us to the Brookland PD?"

Flynn stepped forward. "I'll bring Ms. Templeton and the baby to you. That way, I can take her someplace else when you're finished as she obviously can't stay here."

The officer frowned. "Who are you again?"

"MDP Officer Flynn Ryerson, I work for Rhy Finnegan's tactical team." Dropping his boss's name had the desired effect. The officer straightened and nodded.

"Oh yes, of course. We're familiar with Captain Finnegan. We'll meet you at the Brookland PD." The cop turned away, then paused to glance back at him. "You're not going to call Finnegan, are you?"

"Not at this time," Flynn said. "But depending on what happens next, I may have to." He gestured to the large home. "You do realize he's going to hear about this, as we're only ten blocks from where he lives. This isn't the type of place where people are murdered in their beds."

The cop made a face. "Tell me about it."

Flynn noticed Taylor was shoving more items from the kitchen cupboard into the diaper bag. "Here, you take Max, I'll do that."

"No need. I have it." She used all her weight to press down on the stuff inside. Then she dropped her chin to her chest, heaving a sigh. "I don't know what to do."

He moved closer. "It's going to be okay. We'll get through this by taking one step at a time."

She lifted her head and quickly brushed tears from her eyes. She drew in a shaky breath. "Okay. I'm ready."

"Do you have a coat?" There had been frost warnings in the news, which were not unusual for early November. "And where is the car seat?"

"My coat is in the mud room, and the infant seat is in the Millers' car." She gestured to the right. "They let me use their vehicle at times. Is it okay to go out there? I forgot I wasn't supposed to touch anything."

"You've been living here; your fingerprints are all over the place anyway." He understood Rawson's concern about preserving evidence, but if this was a professional hit, there wouldn't be much of anything to find. "Besides, there's no reason to believe the gunman was in the mudroom or the garage. There's a broken window in the office that faces the back of the house. That appears to be the point of entry."

"Yes, I think so too. I heard the glass breaking." She shivered. "If I hadn't been awake and feeding Max . . ."

"Don't dwell on the what-if scenarios," he advised. "There's no point in looking backward. Let's just grab what we need to get out of here."

She gave a jerky nod and proceeded to the mudroom, which served as a first-floor laundry room as well. After donning a puffy navy-blue winter coat, she opened the garage door and flicked on the light.

He continued holding Max until she had the car seat out of the vehicle and sitting on the dryer. She rummaged in the diaper bag for a blanket, then took Max from his arms. With deft movements, Taylor buckled the sleeping baby into the car seat, then tucked the blanket around him for added warmth.

"I'll take that." He reached for the car seat. "My car is out front. Stay close to me, okay?"

"You don't think the killer is still out there, do you?" Taylor's blue eyes widened with apprehension.

"Not likely, but humor me." Flynn still experienced a stab of guilt over the way he'd inadvertently put his teammate in danger by trusting the wrong man. That had been almost a year ago, and he'd done his best not to let that slip paralyze him moving forward. Rhy had been unwaveringly supportive about the whole debacle. Still, Flynn tended to be more cautious these days.

He didn't want to make another mistake like that ever again.

Red and blue lights lit up the sky from the three responding squads parked in front of the house. Flynn fully expected more to arrive, along with the crime scene techs who would be tasked with collecting evidence from the house. The ME would be called in, too, even though there was no question about the cause of death. His black SUV was parked behind the squads as he'd pulled up a minute after the officers.

And had been extremely upset that they hadn't breached the house prior to his arrival. He'd taken the lead, kicking the front door in to gain access, even as the other officers had yelled for him to stay back.

Now those same officers gave him room to move past them mostly out of respect for Rhy Finnegan, rather than for him specifically. He opened the rear passenger door and grimaced at the garbage that littered the back seat.

"Do you live in your car or what?" Taylor asked, eyeing the mess.

"No. Sorry." His reputation for being a slob hadn't bothered him until now. With quick movements, he brushed the fast-food bags and crumpled napkins to the floor. Then he set Max's car seat down on the cushion.

"I'll do it." Taylor pushed him aside. "I suspect the front seat doesn't look much better."

Since she was right about that, he stepped back and opened the front passenger door to clean off the seat for her. He took a moment to shove as much of the garbage into one of the larger fast-food bags as possible to minimize the mess.

Still, there was no way to get rid of it all. Other than tossing what was left onto the floor of the front seat into the back.

Yeah, he really needed to do a better job of cleaning up after himself.

When that was finished, he took a moment to put Taylor's suitcase in the back before sliding in behind the wheel.

"Good grief," Taylor muttered as she settled into the newly cleared away passenger seat. She glanced at him with exasperation as she clicked her seatbelt into place. "I don't even want to imagine what your house looks like."

He shrugged as he started the engine. "It's not that bad."

"Yeah, why don't I believe that?" Her tone was lightly sarcastic, and he was glad she was thinking about something other than the brutal murders. Then as he pulled away from the curb, she asked, "How long will this take?"

"I'm not sure." He glanced at her. "I guess that depends on what you know about what happened."

She frowned. "I have no idea why someone broke into the house to murder the Millers. They're decent people from what I know. I've only been here for two weeks, but they've been nice enough. Not as demanding as some new parents I've worked with."

"You texted me that you were hiding in the closet," he said. "Was that after you heard the gunfire?"

"I'm not sure. Wait, yes, I think so." She shivered. "It all happened so fast. I heard the glass break first. Then the creak of the stairs. I left the nursery with Max to go into my room so I could grab my phone."

"Go on," he said when she paused.

"I hid in the closet, then considered the possibility I was being overly paranoid. I thought maybe Steve had accidentally dropped a glass of water and was returning to his room. I was about to step out of the closet when I heard the four gunshots." She drew in a ragged breath. "I froze, and that's when I saw him. The gunman walked right past my room."

"Wait, you saw him?" Flynn gaped at her. "You saw his face?"

"From the side, yes. He had a big nose and a beard." She scrubbed her hands over her face. "I shrank back into the closet and texted you. I was afraid he'd hear me or the operator if I called 911."

He nodded absently, still reeling from the fact that she saw the perp's face. Or rather, the side of his face. Then a horrible thought struck. "Did he see you?"

"I don't think so." She frowned. "He looked around using a flashlight, but then left. I don't think he'd have walked away if he'd caught a glimpse of me hiding in the closet."

"No, probably not." Still, Flynn didn't like it. If the perp had swept his flashlight over the room, he had to have noticed the empty but obviously slept-in bed. He'd have to assume someone had been staying there.

"I heard the police sirens shortly after that," Taylor said. "I figured the sound scared him away."

"I'm sure it did." The news was hardly reassuring. The gunman had killed two people in their beds. Was it possible the perp had the means to learn that the Millers had hired a live-in nanny?

If so, Taylor Templeton could very well be next on the killer's hit list.

9 781962 275255